Alice Werner

A Time and Times

Ballads and Lyrics of East and West

Alice Werner

A Time and Times
Ballads and Lyrics of East and West

ISBN/EAN: 9783744776868

Printed in Europe, USA, Canada, Australia, Japan

Cover: Foto ©Andreas Hilbeck / pixelio.de

More available books at **www.hansebooks.com**

A TIME AND TIMES

BALLADS AND LYRICS

OF

EAST AND WEST

——o——

By A. WERNER
Author of " The King of the Silver City "

——o——

' Ich aber will auf mich raffen,
Mein Saitenspiel in der Hand,—
Die Weiten der Erde durchschweifen,
Und singen von Land zu Land.'

ıCHAMISSO

London

T. FISHER UNWIN
26 PATERNOSTER SQUARE

1886

To my friends at St. Andrews.

ἢ μεγάλα χάρις
δώρῳ συν ὀλίγῳ · πάντα δὲ τίματα τά πάρ φίλων.

THEOCRITUS.

NEW YEAR, 1886.

PREFACE.

Most of these poems have already appeared
as fugitive pieces in various British and
American periodicals. Three only are copy-
right—the 'Song of a Singer,' and the
'Mermaid of Zennor,' being reprinted from
Every Girls' Magazine, by kind permission of
Messrs. George Routledge & Sons, and
'Bannerman of the Dandenong' from the
People's Friend, by that of Messrs. John Leng
and Co., Dundee.

St. Andrews,
December 26th, 1885.

CONTENTS.

1885.

IS the time evil?   Who shall tell?
   Is it a good time?   Dare we say?
We hear afar the surges swell—
   Before the coming tempest sway
   The tree-tops—yet the thunders stay.

A day of storm—an age of strife
   Comes up, when all things shall be tried—
And old things purged to better life,
   And base things known and cast aside,
   Among the nations far and wide.

Why tremble at the light of day,
   Or winds of God that sweep the earth?
'Tis but the False they bear away,—
   The True stands storm and fire: all worth
   Shines glorified at dawn's new birth.

DAWN.

IT comes—it looms up in the darkness—
  Something :—I hardly know
Of a word, or a name to name it ;—
  But I feel it must be so ;
That a time of choice is coming
  For weal or for woe.

The pulses of a nation
  Beating in fever and pain :
The fever of woe and want—
  The fever of greed and gain,—
And the stars are reeling in heaven—
  And the great sea moans for her slain.

In the stillness of my life,
  I hear the tramp afar
Of the armies marching,
  Under the morning star,
To the Armageddon battle,
  Where the eagles are.

The days lie dark before me :—
  I know not what shall be,
But at midnight or at day-dawn,
  When the call comes unto me,
I am ready to rise and follow—
  To the death-agony.

B

O my people, my brothers!
  God grant me to be true—
Ever true to His highest truth!—
  No great thing can I do:—
But, firm as a faithful heart may love,
  Ever I stand by you.

Yours:—and I see God's angel
  Coming along the sky,
With the garments rolled in blood,
  And the steadfast eye—
And some say her name is Love,
  And some, Liberty.

She comes—who will know her coming?
  Or be ready her step to greet,
When she comes with the blood on her brow
  And the dust about her feet?
Who will bravely drink of the bitter
  Without a hope of the sweet?

Let us be true—heart-loyal—
  Ready what time she calls!
Justice and Truth are met
  To cast down the age-built walls.
Happy shall be the victors that day,
  And blessed he who falls!

THE HYMN OF HUMANITY.

HUMANITY ! Humanity !
 "Mother, O Mother !" thy children cry,
Stretching out weary, wasted hands
Over the tawny desert sands,—
" Weak and helpless, and very lone,—
Come unto us thine own, thine own !
We stumble and stray in the burning heat,
Blinded our eyes, and scorched our feet !
We have lost our way, and our strength is gone,—
We cannot take one step farther on ;—
Mother—O Mother, hear our cry !—
We hunger and thirst, and we shall die ! "

Humanity ! Humanity !
She heard in the desert her children's cry—
Wildly she moaned and wrung her hands,
And sat her down on the weary sands,
" Alas ! my children, that cry on me !
There is no help in Humanity ! "

Humanity ! Humanity !—
The wail of her pain went up on high :
She cast the sand on her stricken head,
And wept and would not be comforted.
" I cannot help you, my own, my own !
Myself am weary, and weak, and lone,—
Sick and wounded, and like to die ! "—
Humanity ! Humanity !

Humanity ! Humanity !
She cried in her bitter agony—
"No helper--none!—and I called to ye,
My children—and none can answer me !
The chains are sore on my hands and feet,
And I looked for help—and hope was sweet,—
But I waited long, and none came to me ! "—
Humanity ! Humanity !

"Humanity ! Humanity !
She sat in the desert, and One came by,
Into whose footsteps the blood-drops ran,—
And his face was like to a Son of Man.
"Come, thou weary, I heard thy cry,—
I have suffered thine agony !
Stand up, stand up in thy liberty,
And look to the Christ that healeth thee ! "—
Who even Himself is a child of thee—
Humanity ! Humanity !

Humanity ! Humanity !
Shall not her children hear her cry ?
The chains have dropt from her feet and hands,
As she walketh over the desert sands,
And on the track where He went before
The rose and myrtle spring evermore.
"Follow, follow the Son of God !
There is hope and help in the path He trod !
Call unto Him, and not to me ! "
Humanity ! Humanity !—

AMERICA.

O MIGHTY land of pulses young !
  O great heart beating warm and strong !
Now the old feuds are laid to rest
'Twixt English of the East and West ;

And we, of older race on earth,
Watch proud your glories in their birth,
And cry across the seas to you,
" Faint not, fail not, be pure and true !"

The trust we scantly did fulfil,
With clearer eye and stronger will,
Take up ; and, where we fell, stand fast,
Made wiser by our losses past.

The brightness of the old-world years,
The gain of all past strifes and tears,
The strength hard-won in conflicts sore—
These shall be yours for evermore.

Yours be the Spartan constancy,
The Roman might of victory,
And majesty of rule and law,—
The Saxon simple heart of awe.

And, gathering up from every age
The great and good for heritage,
Write ye aloft your country's name,
Purged from all youthful sin and blame.

That, as she sits betwixt the seas,
We yet may gather round her knees,
Learning, in simpleness and truth ;
And find again our own lost youth.

O Glorious !— across the sea
What can our spirit cry to thee?
Hand on the lamp to ages new—
Be true—to thine own self be true !—.

QUEEN LOVE.

"And when she bids die, he shall surely die
Yea he shall leave all things under the sky,
And go forth naked under sun and rain,
And work, and wait, and watch out all his years."

A. C. SWINBURNE. *(The Pilgrims.)*

H E is young, and the sunshine on his hair,
He looks round, dreaming:—" The world is fair."

He feels her hand on his shoulder laid,
Her deep eyes ask him, " Art thou afraid ? "

They smite him, sword-wise. " Who art thou ?—tell ! "
" Ask thine own heart—thou knowest me well.

" Didst thou not call me in dreams of youth ?
Wilt thou not follow in very truth ? "

" Yes, I know thee, and fair art thou,
But let me linger a little now.

" Youth comes but once, and life is sweet,
Thorny and steep are the ways of thy feet."

" Yea, in sooth ! " made answer she,
" Else had I never callèd thee."

" Not yet—not yet ! " he cried with a groan.
" To face the world and stand forth alone ! "

" Those whom I love must ever be
Hated of men for the love of me."

"But there are near and dear ones," he cried,—
"Father and mother, and tender bride :

"Leave me a little, till they can know,
And so the parting be less of woe."

Tender and stern grew the eyes whose dole
Pierced into his very soul.

"Nay," she answered, "it may not be.
They must yield all, who follow me.

"If I leave thee, thou canst not be
Light of heart—for thou lovest me.

"And the love thou canst not forget will be
Lifelong torment of hell for thee."

He said, as one drowning gasps for breath,
"I follow thee to the bitter death."

He heard them calling, "Stay, oh! stay!"
He turned his face to the desert way.

With bare feet set on the burning sands,
Sadly he loosened the clasping hands.

A nameless joy, and a nameless woe
Strove at his heart :—"Ye must let me go."

Betwixt her two hands she took his face,
And kissed his lips for a crowning grace.

Now I know thou art truly mine!
Go forth on thy way, through storm and shine.

" Perchance thou shalt see me never again,
It may be not even in dying pain,—

" But know thou, in sorrow and blackness of night,
Thou art doing my work, and hast chosen the right.

" Doubt not, faint not ; thy guerdon shall be,
This, that thou diest at last for me."

POET AND REPUBLICAN.

I.

H E lay upon the thymy down
　　The summer sky was soft above,—
'Mid hare-bells blue and grass-plumes brown,
　　He mused high thoughts of faith and love.

And fainter hummed the bees about
　　His ear, and fainter grew the sky ;
He seemed to hear the battle-shout,
　　And see the hosts go sweeping by.

And down, and dale, and summer day
　　Became a glorious dream to him
Of great deeds dared and done,—while lay
　　Helpless his form, with sealed eyes dim.

At even, he awoke, and there
　　Found himself lying in the thyme,
And saw afar,—so pure and fair,
　　The skyward hills that he must climb.
Alas ! Alas ! the dream that was !
　　The listless frame and life sublime !—

II.

A couch within a fair, large room—
Through tinted window-panes, the light
Fell softly in a purple gloom,
And all things round were fair and bright.

Rich forms and hues where'er he turned,—
The peacock's feather drooped above,—
And Clytie's face down on him burned
Out of its yearning depths of love.

And, in the streets, the throbbing cries
Of human life that never rest—
They brought no flash into his eyes
Nor any trouble to his breast.

He lay there, stringing rhyme on rhyme
Of liberty, and love, and pain,
And all the sorrows of the time,—
And turned himself to dream again . . .
Alas! Alas! the dream that was!
Must high dreams always be in vain?

NAPOLEON:

Two Sonnets.

"Je le croyais fait pour quelque chose de mieux."—P. L. Courier.

I. On Board the Bellerophon.

FALLEN ! O thou from whom we hoped such things !
    Thou ! set to be the People's guiding star . . . .
O beautiful face that lighted us from far,
Crowned with a better glory than of kings !—
About thy straying feet our spirit clings
    In spite of all—Oh ! why didst thou so mar
    The life that might have been, and set a bar
Betwixt thy soul and her celestial springs ?
This is a lesser fall we now behold,
    But not for that less bitter ;—nay, for now
    Surely, that agony of lip and brow
Is most the memory of that uncontrolled
Passion, that took the first false step aside . . . . .
Oh ! that thou hadst been true,—and we had died !—

II. In the Invalides.

The haunting love that will not let thee rest
    Clings yet about thy great heart in his grave ;
    Methinks that, where men's souls their just meed have,
This love of all thy pangs is cruellest.

Oh ! thou wast made for greatest and for best,
   Made to be loved, and love, and serve, and save
   Thy France, and Europe—not to be a slave
To that false fame by this world's kings possest.
Thy great deeds planned thou seest brought to nought,—
   Thy clear-eyed wisdom, folly,—and thy strength
   Weak in His hands who made all things to be,—
The People cheated of their hope,—each thought
Bitter in turn—but bitterest this at length—
"This love, this love it is that tortures me !"—

IN THE LATTER DAYS.

O MY people, my people ! the curtains of night are
drawn,—
But, looking up, I can see through the rifts the breaking
of the dawn.

O my people, my people ! ye have been patient long,
But the race is not to the swift, nor the battle to the
strong ;

And the shoulders bowed with the burden, and the eyes
that ache for tears,
Shall have their turn for rest and joy, in the coming
years.

O my people, my people ! I would help you, but I am
weak :
I am not a prophet, nor worker, nor one to whom men
might seek,

To save them in their need, or lead them on to the
fight :
But God hath said to me *I am*, and there shall be Light.

O my people, my people ! when days are dark in the sky,
And the great world spins on aimless, and we wish for
naught but to die,

It is then that I would tell you—I, who have known the
pain
Of the horrible, desolate darkness, and shuddered and
struggled in vain,

Who have looked to one man and another, would
have given the heart from my breast. . . .
And felt the earth stagger beneath me when he failed
and fell like the rest,—

How we have a Leader, a hero, the man for whom men's
souls long,—
Man whom men's hearts may trust in, pure, and tender,
and strong.

Man of men, our Brother, He stands in the holiest place,
But its glory has not driven the shadow of earth from
His face.

He is sad for the cry of his brothers, when they think
that wrong prevails,
And the right hand that guides the stars is scarred with
the print of the nails.

Say that man cannot rise ? Do we not know he can,
When the Everlasting Righteousness has worn the face
of a man ?

And while that Man stands in heaven, we know, be it
slow or fast,
That every soul of man shall rise to be what He is at last.

O my people, my brothers ! if he be with us indeed,
What matter how sore the struggle ? We follow where
he shall lead.

And the joy of earth is coming,—I hear her feet on Life's
shore,
And all shall be well, as the Highest hath willed it, for
evermore.

A DEMAGOGUE'S WISH.

" WHAT do I wish for myself? " he said,
      And a strange wild light broke over his face,—
" What do I wish when the work's all sped :—

" The cheer on cheer of the market-place,
      And thousands of faces burning bright
With the light of a people's love and praise ?

" Or the calm, sweet days, when faith is sight,
      And the battle over, and Life drawn on
Peacefully towards Death's restful night ?

" Or just to be borne forth when all is done,
      With tired hands laid still on my breast,
And eyes too weary to see the sun,

" 'Mid a people's mourning unto my rest ?—
      —No—not quite,—though once I deemed so,—
This have not even the bravest and best.

" Not this I wish :—I have lived, and I know.
      But, when I have wrung out my heart's best blood
In work for the world,—and have known the woe

" Of the world's worst pain,—and have done what good
      I can,—and they hate me too in their turn—
Would I cheat them of their love, if I could ?—

"Why, then, let the hard words begin to burn,
  And stones to fly, and muskets to flash :—
To die that way I suppose one can learn ;—

"And while the roar of the blind, mad crash
  Spends itself—one or two true ones, I know,
Would lay the bruised limbs where cool waves plash,

" To sleep in God's earth. . .   And then they would
  grow
  To freedom and truth, and righteousness on,
Forgetting the heart that loved them so . . .
  That's what I wish," he said, " when all's done."—

A FAREWELL.

April 5th, 1884.

"Prepare yourselves for a settlement of this question. It must come up for settlement sooner than you are prepared for it, and the sooner you commence that preparation the better for you."
John Brown of Osawatomie.

THE world was sad, and the age was late : —
A man went out from the Western Gate.

He passed through the streets, where young and old
Thrust and tore in the strife for gold ;

And sad, starved faces, fevered and thin,
Were as a circle to wall him in.

And he cried aloud in his sorrow of heart,
" Is there never a better part ?

" Must it be so to the end of time
For the many who sink and the few who climb ?

" Were not all things made good ? Should gain
Come to you from your brother's pain ? "

So, with his faith in God above,
And his hope for man, and his passing love,

Eastward he passed, and his deep words came
Thrilling men's hearts with a touch of flame.

He came to our land across the sea :—
"O heart of man ! there is joy for thee !

" Why droop thy heavy eyes to the sod ?
Look up—have hope in thyself and God.

" Moan no longer for what might be :
Take thy birthright, and stand up free."

We heard him speak, and a wind went forth
Over the land to south and north.

A voice as of sea-waves that leap and hiss :
And England, hearing, asks, " What is this ? "

Lo ! this is a thing thou hast not seen
In all thine ages, O Island-Queen !

Hearken, O ear, and look, O eye—
Lest the day of thy glory pass thee by.

Over the length and breadth of the land
There are some who listen and understand.

Call to her, true hearts ! bid her awake,
Stand, and strive truly for Love's dear sake.

And for thee, who hast left us . . . . The seed is sown :
We will think of thee when the trees are grown.

Our thanks—what are they ?—but over the sea
One last greeting we send to thee.

Thanks, and greeting from all that have blest
God who sent thee out of the West.

" In thoughts from the visions of the Night."

THOU who art cunning of hand to paint,
    Paint me my dream that came in the night—
Vision that was so blessed and bright,
Only words, mere words are too faint,
    If I would try to tell it aright.

A deep blue sky, and a southern sea,
    With its passionate sapphire and crystal spray,
    In the brooding light of a golden day,—
This is what seemèd unto me,—
    And wild rocks, jagged, and black and grey.

And in the midst of the bay was set
    A grand, great image of marble white,
    Of stature more than man's to the sight ;—
Round his feet the wavelets rippled and met,
    Flowing and flashing in dazzling light.

And a beautiful face, with straining eyes,
    All upturned to the glowing sky,—
    And parted lips for a yearning cry
Of the soul that longeth to be made wise,—
    And hands, palm upwards, lifted on high.

Away from the tides that ebb and flow,—
    Away from the lights which darken and fade,—
    From Earth in her changing beauty arrayed,—
From the lives of men that come and go,—
    To That which was before all was made.

MY SWORD.

M Y sword! thou art bright—thou art keen !
The flash of thee sendeth a thrill
Through mind, and spirit, and will—
Thou long'st for the battle I ween ?
Long, long, hast thou been lying by—
When shall we arise, thou and I,
And strike in the cause of the Lord,
My sword ?

My sword !—my good sword and true !—
Yea, I know thou art surely mine
In right of a gift divine
For ever to dare and to do,—-
Mine to draw from my side,
And hew down the strong in his pride,—
Sin and wrong, and their barbarous horde—
My sword !—

My sword !—as I open the chest,
And throw back the mantles that cover
Thy glorious brightness over,
And draw thee forth from thy rest—
I long for the time to come
To hear the roll of the drum,
The trump, and the Captain's word,
My sword !

My sword!—yet, oft, as I gaze,
 My eyes grow dim with tears,
 And a rush of surging fears
Wraps all in a blinding haze.
  Art thou true, my blade untried?
  Is it only my foolish pride
  That sees thy flashing light?
  How wilt thou stand the fight
  Mid the hail of blows forth poured,
   My sword?

O sword!—and though thou be strong
 And faithful—yet in the field
 How shall this poor arm wield
Thee worthily 'mid the throng?
  When the battle's press is sore,
  And a long, long day before,
  And even the heart within
  Beset with sorrow and sin,—
  'Tis not for me thou art stored—
   O sword!

Nay, nay—my sword—thou art mine!
 The Father that gave thee to me,
 Will grant thee faithful to be,
And grant me His strength divine—
  So forth we go to the fight,
  Armed in the power of His might—
  Together, thou and I,
  Till the evening draweth nigh,
  And we kneel at the feet of the Lord—
   My sword!—

AFTER A WEEK IN TOWN.

January 20th, 1884.

BACK again !—from the mist and the whirl,
    The joy and the pain of London Street,
To the dark, still river with oily swirl,—
    In the evening air that is fresh and sweet.

A grand calm planet shines out in the sky,
    'Mid the chasing clouds that haste from the West,—
The gulf of a life-time seems to lie
    Between : yet scarce more than a week at best

Since I trod the pavement last. How still,
    Sleepy almost, the old town seems : —
And the stir, and tumult, and voices shrill
    Behind me are but a whirl of dreams.

Which are the dreams, and which is the waking ?
    May be 'tis London's sorrow and strife,—
Not the peace here, that goes to the making
    Up of one's real, work-a-day-life.

Back—yes, I'm glad to be back again ;—
    Kensington lay like a load on my breast,
And the lights, and noise, and the whirl and strain,—
    I cannot bear it—I long for rest.

Kensington ! with the stately streets,—
    The grey, gaunt houses, ghastly and grim,
Empty and echoing,—and the sheets
    Of the fog drawn over them, grey and dim.

A great, dead city it seemed to me—
Like one in a dream I walked therein,
And the sky, and the earth, and the smoke-slain tree
Seemed crying, crying of want and sin.

And phantom-shadows the fair ones all
That passed so sweet and so smiling there ;—
Behind them a spectre rose—bitter as gall,
Gaunt as famine, white as despair.

Back again—where the air is purer,—
Where men's faces can gather light
From the stainless sky·—where earth seems surer,
And less hides God from our spirits' sight.

And yet—and yet—Is it strange ?—is it wrong,
That from all that's soothing to heart and brain,.
From the sweet, pure country, I yet should long
Back to the sad, great city again ?

Sad mother-city, weariful London,
Restless with pain as the sobbing sea,
What shall be done to us if we leave undone
Aught of the duty we owe to thee ?

Life may be bright in the far lands golden :
London ! London ! I strive in vain
To 'scape the voice of thy sorrows olden,
It will not out of my ears again !

NINETEENTH CENTURY IDEALS.

" I HAVE an ideal "—you say
"But I know not what I will ? "—
Ah me! I long for the Kingdom of God
  That shall do away all ill.

But what to wish for I know not,
  Nor know I how it shall be :
All around me I see the world
  Heave like the surging sea.

My faith is in holy freedom—
  But till men are true and strong,
No need to tell me it only means
  Freedom to do the wrong . . . .

The work must be done some day,—
  And it will be done, no doubt.
But what is best to wish for meanwhile
  Is past my finding out.

Would a Republic help us
  If men were the same as now ?
Or would the nation's ills be cured
  If all had lands to plough.

One only thing I see clearly
  In this waste of sorrow and sin—
And that is the fight which each man has
  To fight for the Kingdom within.

Perhaps, when we've won that battle
Which takes a life-time to win,
It may become somewhat clearer
How the Kingdom on earth's to begin.

Meanwhile we have flowers and sunshine,
And a poor soul here and there
Whom a word or look may bring nearer
To all things great and fair.

There are waves and woods and meadows,
And winds and skies above,
And the wondrous world of living things
Whom the great God doth love.

There are little children to love—
There is work, to do one's best :—
Is not that enough for a lifetime?
And let God take the rest!

SONNET.

METHOUGHT I saw a dark, defiant face,
With fierce lips set in everlasting scorn,
And backward-blown wild locks by storm-blasts torn,
Sad eyes, deep-caverned—not without the grace
Of tenderness, that found no resting-place
  In that despairing world, whereinto born,
  He knew not how to make it less forlorn,—
And so defied, and died : men call him base.

I saw this man : before his feet there knelt
  A hunted, haggard slave with fettered limb,
  And branded cheek. "Nay—what is mine is thine !"—
Smiled he, and raising, flung an arm round him.
" *Who art thou ?* " And before I heard, I felt
His answer—" *Lucius Sergius Catiline.*"

IN A CONCERT ROOM.

HOW my whole heart yearns out to you,
O dark-eyed Singer, with the face
To light a nation on to dare
All at one blow,—though poor and few!—
I thank you, thank you for this grace,
That are so far above me there.

I do not envy you the gift
That was not given to me, who know
No secrets of the tunèd chord,
Nor half can tell, when you uplift
The souls of men and women so,
The meaning in your music stored.

You soar aloft on wings of song,
So high above our dull, poor life
Of struggles vain, ideals lost,
And slothful yielding to the wrong,—
Of high aims lowered,—petty strife,—
And hands, of love that count the cost.

The words, that fall so dead and cold
From lips like ours, you breathe like flame—
They glow and fall in flakes of fire
On men enwrapt in lust of gold,
And counting goodness but a name,—
Crusted in this world's foulest mire.

No spirit you—a woman true,
    With warm heart-pulse that beats and burns,—
      And yet no woman man may love ;
No angel calm, for, through and through,
    The human soul within you yearns
      With the same thoughts in us that move.

And yet a scarcely human thing—
    A star—a glowing sunlight-streak
      Upon a sea—sent down to bless :
For none of those that hear you sing
    Shall clasp your neck, or kiss your cheek,—
      Yet all love you,—nor can you less

Than love them all.   Your heart is wide,
    And holds of love as 'twere a sea
      That cannot be poured out on one,
But must seek all in fullest tide .   .   .   .
    Unless one formed for you, maybe,
      Wait in the worlds beyond the sun.

Let me look up into your eyes ! ·
    I may not ask to touch your hand—
      Only to bless you for this night !
I pray, in dark hours there may rise,
    As dreams to comfort you, the band
      Of souls to whom you brought the light.

CALABRIA ULTRA, 1863.

I 'M only a peasant of Bova, —a poor wild lad of the hills—
I know how to shoot the wild deer, and train the stock of the vine,
And climb the paths of the mountains, and track the course of the rills,—
And yonder cabin, and this, my rifle, are all that is mine.

I've nought in the world to be proud of—I thought so once, long ago,—
But now all the years of my life show wretched and selfish and mean ;—
I can't just tell you, Signore,—you who are learned must know . . . .
But since *he* came here,—things seemed different to what they had ever been. . . .

Did I know him ? Know him ! I followed him hence when he came—
Marched to Napoli with him—fought within sight of his eye,—
Lay in a hospital, wounded, and weak, and weary, and lame,—
Felt his smile rest on me, and was all too happy to die.

Brave was I ?—No Signore—I only followed where he
Led us—as indeed such as I might follow afar ;—
Only as they are brave, who, lost in the mountains, can see
High in the heavens, and follow their glorious guiding-star.

Love him ? Ah Signore—do you in your cold fog-land
  Know what love means? And yet methinks some of
  you know it well ;
There were Englishmen there, 'mid the bravest of the
  band,
    Fought beside us like brothers, and looked to *him*
    when they fell.

If they are all like those in that far-away England of
  yours,
  Ah !—what a land it must be, so noble and true and
  brave—
Great, warm hearts in plenty, to gladden the cold, bleak
  shores !—
    Blessed land !—But why do you turn your head, and
    look grave ?

Where is Caprera, Signore? I heard them say in the
  town
  He was gone to stay there, till he came to lead us
  once more ;—
Can you tell in what province ?—and is it a long way
  down
    Here from the mountains? Out yonder lies Reggio
    down by the shore,

(Only you cannot see it from here),—is it over that way ?
  Or is it far beyond Napoli there by the sea ?—
If I might herd his goats, or seek his lambs when they
  stray,
    I were content—do you think he would be much
    troubled with me ?—

Till we march on Rome, where the Pope and his
  Cardinals live—
  Why do you shake your head—and say it will never
    be ?—
He lives still, our Hero—why, he has only to give
  The word,—our thousands stand ready to follow, by
    land or sea.

Scorn him—you say some do—and call him dreamer and
    fool ?
  Don't tell me so, Signore—I know that it cannot be—
Hate him they may—the priests and monks all do, as a
    rule—
  Padre Francesco up there, for instance—but don't tell
    me !—

Scorn him ? I'd like to see the man who thought to do
    so !
  Ah ! they will find out yet he knows far better than
    they !—
You and I, Signore,—you're one of the right sort, I know,
  By the light in your eyes when you named him—God
    grant we may see the day !—

Talk of him *so*, do they ? I wish they were here just
    now ! . . . .
  And yet—poor souls, they don't know him, or know
    what is true and right . . . .
He said we were to love each other, as *CHRIST* showed
    us how . . . .
  This is the road, Signore, and there's Mileto in sight.

UNDER SENTENCE.

MILAN, 185—.

THIS night's my last !
All life's struggle over and past,—
Yet I scarce can call it a battle won—
What have I done ?

Twenty-three years
Lived out in doubts and hopes and fears ;—
Poor, faint, broken, half-hearted Past—
So crowned at last ?

I know what shall be
When they have loaded the carbines for me :
I know a place in the city square—
I shall stand there.

A flash and a crash—
And a sound in my ears of dark waves that dash,—
And all will be over—and I in the light
Where all is made right.

And that this should be I,
Who was not worthy for her to die !—
I to be one of thy martyr-band—
O our glorious land ?—

D

The summer morn
From the night's clear depths again is born ;
Golden the eastern sky glows there—
    The day will be fair . . .

The hour is come,
With the clash of steel and the roll of drum :—
The carbines are loaded, and waiting for me—
    I shall soon be free.

For the joy of this hour :—
For the guiding arm of Thy love and power :—
For the future that glows—for the strength that
    sufficed—
    I bless thee—O Christ !—

INNOMINATA.

L AY her down in the foreign land,—
   Bring the flowers to lay on her breast,—
Lilies for maidenhood,—roses for love;
Only here, in the little right hand,
   Clasp her the blossoms she loved the best—
   Violets, blue as her skies above.

Only a young maid of nineteen years—
   Yet true a martyr as ever bled
      For freedom and truth in the long ago ;
By her smile, when those bright eyes ached for tears,
   By sorrow dumb, she has earned that red
      Dark rose on her death-robe white as snow.

She stood up straight in her young life's light,
   With white, soft feet unshrinkingly set
      On the sharp-stoned way that the great ones trod.
" Italy ! Italy ! " Full on her sight
   Glowed the vision, unseen as yet
      Unto all but the Called of God.

She took up the burden with gladsome heart
   Of loyal duty, and held it up
      In those two slim hands that ached with the strain ;
Steadily bearing, through joy or smart,
   As a crystal holy-water-cup,
      That must be borne without spilling or stain.

But the way was long and the burden sore,
  And spirit was strong, but flesh was weak,
    And her heart just broke without ever a cry ;
And tightly her fingers closed once more
  Round the cup, and the rose-red fell from her cheek
    And she only thought—"It is sweet to die ! "

Roses, red roses of martyrdom,
  Lilies spotless of maidenhood,—
    Lay them tenderly here on her breast,
With the violets meet for a maid of Rome,
  Who, bearing the hard day's burden, stood
    And died at her post ;—so leave her to rest.

CZAR ALEXANDER.

JUNE, 1883.

POOR man, whom we hate in our blindness,
    Because we are too much like thee,—
When shall we have learnt the true kindness
    That maketh men free?
Ages hence they shall tell it in story
    How the pomp of thy crowning was made ;—
Sad heart, 'mid the blaze of thy glory,
    Art thou not afraid ?

When thousands around thee were kneeling,
    And the sound of the chanting was still,
And earth's mightiest empire was feeling
    The might of thy will,—
When they brought forth the diadem mystic,
    No hand sets on thee but thine own,—
And the priest poured the Wine Eucharistic
    For one man alone,—

Did the light never dazzle and blind thee— ·
    The loneliness sicken and scare ?
All alone on thy height shall God find thee—
    No creature else there ?
Cut off from all fellowship human,
    Unhelped by divine—who can be
Near God, far from man and from woman ?—
    Shall none pity thee ?

And then . . . Does that low, circling thunder
    Wake aught in thy soul but a fear   '
And thought of self-saving ? I wonder,
    As nearer and near
The lightnings are playing and flashing,
    And the cloud-piles drift onward and meet,
And the tide-wave of Nations is dashing
    Unawed round thy feet.

Didst thou think of the millions about thee,
    The worshipping, ignorant souls,
Whose lives were as nothing without thee,
    Whose prayer for thee rolls
In a stream never-ceasing to heaven ?
    Or those sad, steadfast thousands, whose breath
Were this moment ungrudgingly given
    To purchase thy death ?

There is nothing can hinder or stay them,
    Nor pity nor fear do they know :
They care not for thee, though thou slay them
    In bitterest woe.
Thou hast sinned in the name of the Highest,—
    They tread down the kingdoms and creeds,
Denying the God thou deniest
    By voice of thy deeds.

Oh ! the heaped up transgressions of ages
    That weigh down the crown on thy head !
The sins of thy fathers—the wages
    Of sinners long dead !

And the hour and the doom that delay not
    Are coming—no help is for thee
From thy bayonet-millions, that stay not
    The Eternal Decree.

O Man, first of all men in sorrow,
    Because thou art highest in pride !
Men's hearts faint for fear of the morrow,
    The red harvest-tide . . .
Oh ! is there no prophet that waketh,
    To cry from the hill-tops above
And tell us how day-dawning breaketh
    In Justice and Love ?—

GEORGE TINWORTH.

A CRAFTSMAN-ARTIST of the olden time,
Dowered with the cunning hand and reverent eye.
That scorns no meanest thing he passes by,
(For all may be as stairs whereby we climb
Unto the clearest heights of God's sublime,)
Nor proudly draws, feeling himself too high,
Apart from brother men that toil and cry,
Heart-weary still, 'mid Pharaoh's bricks and slime.

O Man and Brother! they that work and love
Have ever their reward, and thou hast thine!
Who works like thee, in simple faithfulness,
Shall look clear-eyed upon the Light Divine,
And, blessing others, win a joy above
Their joy, whom this world rises up to bless.

May, 1883.

A LIFE'S LABOUR.

O life I knew!
O heart so true!

O FRESH young hope! O golden prime!—
This Man—he started to run his race,
With the glow of the sunlight on his face,
To run a-tilt against the time.
All things were wrong, but all should be right
Ere he went to his rest in the cool of night.

This Man—he was but a man, ah me!—
With the heart of gold and the hands of clay,
And the high thoughts that die on the lip away :—
No iron will for the strife had he,—
And yet he could not sink back and rest
With the quiet souls whom the world loves best.

He saw the Good flit ever before,
Like the rainbow afar on the mountains seen,
While the clinging mire of the marsh-flats green
Held fast his feet, tho' he struggled sore,
Till the night came, and, broken and lone,
Weary, to rest he laid him down.

Ah me!—and yet I had rather be
That Man, as I saw him lying
With his blue eyes dim in dying,
And the heart that once beat so high and free
Broken with trusting too much,—than they
Who call him fool, and pass on their way!

O life I knew
O high heart true!

THE BATTLE-FIELD BY SILARUS.

B.C. 70. 72.

'TIS a wild and stormy night
    After the battle-day,—
The clouds are after the moon,
    And the wolf is after the prey ;—
The wind is wet from the sea,
    And the tossing pines make moan,
'Tis a fearsome night for who should be
    On Apennine alone.

Yonder a flame leaps up
    And casts a ruddy gleam
On the grey rock-walls of the hills,
    On the turbid, hurrying stream ;—
'Mid the whirls of pitch-pine smoke
    You can mark it now and then,
How it flashes back from the helmets
    And spears of mailèd men.

Mark them there by the watch-fire
    Those faces browned with war,
Stern, and hard, and reckless,
    And seamed with many a scar ;—
And look out into the darkness—
    And what do we seem to see ?—
Aught—save grim ghosts of larch and pine,
    And clouds that sweep to the lee ?

Oh ! the kindly, shrouding darkness—
    Much it hideth here—
Dead limbs laid in the mountain fern
    Hopeless of tomb or tear.
Slaves and out-cast and desolate,
    Banned by the arm of Rome—
Syrian, Libyan, Greek and Gaul,
    Each one has found his home.

Oh ! the pitiful Night is come,
    The gentle voiceless Mother, .
That kisses because she cannot speak :
    There is not such another !
She hath lapt them in soft arms,
    And folded them close to her breast :
She has taught them the thing they knew not
    For now they know what is Rest.

The maimed limbs bare and bleeding—
    The pangs and shame untold,
She hath covered up with her mantle,
    Shrouded close from the cold
Fierce eyes, and the mocking laughter
    We pass them, one by one,
Seeking still in the darkness
    Him whose work is done.

Where the slain lie thickest
    We see his face at last,
By the light of a passing moon-glimpse
    Amid the shadows cast ;—

With his tawny curls blood-clotted,
  And the wide eyes staring dumb
Upward still, as they fixed in death—
  Did they look for hope to come?

Those whose hope was none in life
  Around him here they lie,—
Dying, and dead,—they could not save,
  But stood by him to die :—
To-morrow morn, by Silarus,
  The row of crosses grim,—
And the living, agonized faces that look
  On the still, dead face of him !—

Spartacus ! Spartacus !
  The dumb crushed mass, on whom
The conquering Roman set his foot,—
  The million slaves of Rome —
Cried to thee in their sorrow —
  And they callèd not in vain
When they callèd in their pain,—
  And backward through the centuries
They cry to thee again,
  The great heart that yearned out to them,
And ached for all their pain :—
      Spartacus ! Spartacus !
      Come back to us again !

_____

"WHEN THE TOWERS FALL."

THEY were built by the Lords of Wrong,—
The grey old kings of the world,
Long ago.
Frowning they stood, and strong,
And the sea-waves foamed and curled
Down below.

The sea-waves moaned and wept,
And plucked with wild, vain hands
At the shore ;
The sea-winds wailed and swept
Over bitter, desolate lands
Evermore.

" They shall stand for endless years ! "
Moaned a weary multitude
In their pain,
" The mortar tempered with tears,
And the clay that was kneaded with blood
Of men slain ! "

" They shall stand for aye, and shine ! "
Cried the foolish ones and strong,
In their pride ;
" Landmarks of right divine—
Since they have stood so long
Undefied."

Lo! the years haste on, and the days,
  And the fruit still springs from the seed,
               Good or ill :
And the stars go on in their ways,
  And the holy laws decreed
               Work their will.

They shall bring the morning round
  When the light strikes dim and cold,
               And the True
Shall burn up the False ; and the ground
  Shudder with longing to hold
               All things new.

And lo! the children of men
  Shall know of the Hand of God
               Ruling all :
The sun shall be sackcloth then,
  And the moon be dark with blood,
               When they fall !

THE WHITE WITCH OF PERRAN PORTH.

A Ballad of Cornwall.

I.

TAMSON, Tamson Trevenna!
    Open the door to me,
For the storm is moaning up from the west,
    And the fog is thick on the sea.

" Tamson—Tamson Trevenna,
    Witch or none you may be,—
But help me—help, for the love of God !
    Bring my son home to me ! "

Up rose Tamson Trevenna,—
    Came and opened the door :—
Her right hand held the gown to her breast,
    And her black hair fell to the floor.

" Help me, Tamson Trevenna,—
    For he comes not back from the sea !—
And God forgive the cruel words
    That I've ever said to thee ! "

In the door-way stood Tamson,
    And held the lamp in her hand ;
      " Christ God, save now
      By sea and by land ! "

She set the lamp in the window,
    She knelt down on her knee :—
        " *Holy God, that rulest*
        By land, and by sea :—

" *From the breakers on the reef,*
    From the surf upon the sand,—
From storm and lightning, and star-blasting,
    Save by sea and land ! "

Three times she looked towards the land,
    Three times towards the sea,
And cried, " In the Holy Name of Christ,
    Come thou forth with me ! "

And down and over Perran sands,
    And straight along the shore,
They went their way, and with the lamp
    Tamson went before ;—
Nearer and nearer, low and long
    Crept the tide waves' roar.

And round and round the sea-fogs curled,
    In folding wings of white,
And Enstice Carne shook like a leaf,
    In the lone, wild night :—
But firm and fearless the maiden went—
    Turned not to left or right.

And on a sudden she stood still,
  (The sea was moaning high,
But the fog was thick, and they could not see,)
  And held the lamp on high,
And there was a smile upon her lip,
  And a flash in her dark eye.

" Hark !" she said, " he is here !"   .   .
  Hannibal Carne, who lone
Wandered that night on Perran sands,
  Weary and all foredone,

Saw the gleam of the lamp,
  And his mother standing there,—
And a white, white maid, like the clouded moo n,
  In the night of her dark hair.

His mother clasped him in her arms,
  And kissèd him full fain,
But he had looked into Tamson's eyes
  Ere he kissed her back again.

And on the lone, lone Perran sands,
  Close to the tide-waves' roar,
They looked into each other's eyes,
  And loved for evermore.

II.

It fell upon a summer eve,
  When bright were sky and sea,
Tamson Trevenna sat by the door
  With the Book upon her knee.

E

" Hearken, Tamson Trevenna !
   You're a witch, as they say you be,
Though you may call on the name of God,
   And hold the Book on your knee ! "

" What have I done, Dame Enstice,
   That you should speak to me so ? "
" You know full well the ill you've wrought,
   The wrong and the woe ! "

" Nothing I know, Dame Enstice,
   Of wrong done wittingly ! "
" You've witched the heart from out of his breast
And you've witched my son from me.

" Wisht was the night I asked your help
   To find him on Perran shore,—
Better had he been drowned that night
   Than live to be mine no more ! "

" I have cast no spell upon him,—
   Witchcraft is sin, God saith—
Only I love him with a love
   Stronger than life or death."

" Hark to the foul witch-maiden !   .   .   .
   .   .   .   .   .   If maiden indeed thou be—
I say to thee, if thou loose him not,
   God's curse shall rest on thee ! "

"I cannot bid the tides turn back,
　Or slock the sun from the sky ;—
I cannot say I love him not—
　That were a sin and a lie.
For he loves me, and I love him,
　With a love that cannot die!"

III.

Tamson, Tamson Trevenna !—
　'Tis an evil night for thee—
They have come beneath the holy moon
　Thy dying pain to see.

Tamson, Tamson Trevenna !
　Enstice Carne is there,
And Hacky Bodinnar from the mines,
　And wild Mark of Penair,
And every maid that hates thee sore,
　For she knows herself less fair.

They burst abroad the cottage door,—
　Wild was the shouting din ;
They cast the house upon an heap,
　And all that was therein ;
And forthwith they haled her, with intent
　To do their deed of sin.

"Take off, take off the curse, Tamson,
　And they shall let thee free,
And I'll forgive the cruel wrong
　That thou hast done to me!"

Oh ! and bright flashed Tamson's eyes,
  And she lifted up her head :—
"There is no curse in holy love,
  But the blessing of God,"—she said.

They struck at her with cruel hands—
  To the earth they flung her there ;
They dragged her to the Raven's Cliff
  By the long locks of her hair.

Still lay Tamson Trevenna,
  Still as the midnight sea,
And the cloudless moon,—and never a word
  Save " Christ, my God ! " spake she.

" Hark to the witch ! " they cried,—
  And the outstretched arms were strong,—
And the cliffs were steep,—and the waves were deep—
  . . . . . Done was the deed of wrong.

IV.

A south-east gale sprang up that night,
  At the ebb of the tide.
All in the wild, wet dawn afloat,
A drowned maid drifted past Hannibal's boat,
  With both arms flung wide.

•The gown was torn from her white, white breast,
    Blue-bruised were her shoulders bare,
And round and round in a dark, dark cloud
    Floated her long black hair.

And Hannibal caught at the slim, dead hand,
    He caught at the floating gown,
But the wild waves swept her away from him
    As the tide went down.

To the shore stept Hannibal Carne,
    And a changèd man was he.
"Mother, mother, who did this deed ?—
    Mother—tell it to me ! "

Oh ! and away cowered Enstice Carne,
    From the wrath was in his eye :—
"Hannibal, don't thee look at me so,
    Or I shall surely die ! "

Oh ! and away crouched Enstice Carne
    In the darkest of the room,—
Trembled, and moaned with white wrung lips,
    As she had heard her doom.

"She was a witch"—moaned Enstice Carne,
    " And had cast a spell on thee ! "
And he clasped his hands, and looked up at the sky,
    And round upon the sea.

He clasped his hands before his face,
  And to earth he cast him down :—
" Keep my hands from my mother's life,
  And let me take my own ! "
          *   *   *

Up rose Hannibal Carne from the earth,
  And grim of face was he :
He looked not to the right nor left,
  To land nor to sea ;—
He went to Perran Church on the sands,
  And knelt down on his knee :—
" Hear me, O Christ of the five red wounds !
  Judge betwixt them and me !

" Hear me, hear, O pitying Christ !
  Vengeance belongs to thee !
Tamson Trevenna's a saint in heaven,
  And earth is hell to me !
But hear my vow before I go,
  O Lord, that died on tree :—
Home nor mother nor kin of mine
  Ever more will I see ! "

Oh ! and up rose Hannibal Carne,
  And went forth in his pain
From Perran Church upon the sands
Across the sea to far-off lands,
  And ne'er was seen again.

THE WRECKER'S DAUGHTER.

THE west wind moans, the breakers roar—
   She stands within the cottage door—
"Show the light upon the shore—
         O Meraud!"

There as in a dream she stands,—
Fluttering hair and outstretched hands—
Sees the waves race o'er the sands,—
         Bright Meraud.

Laughing in a girlish glee
At the raging of the sea ;—
Playmate of the storm-winds free
         Is Meraud.

Down beside Carn Barra Bay,
Where the reefs are low and grey,
Waits her father for the prey—
         "Haste, Meraud!"

Where the cliff-path's sharp and steep,
Small bare feet can cling and creep ;
So, through rains and winds that sweep,
         Speeds Meraud.

Where the sharp-fanged rocks lie low,
Hiss the foam-drifts white as snow
Round a ship in her last woe—
         O Meraud !

Every timber strains and shrieks—
Wild-eyed men with haggard cheeks
Reck not when their captain speaks—
    O Meraud!

'Mid the breakers on the lee
Flashed a light :—the foam-flakes flee,
Whirled like lost souls o'er the sea,
    Round Meraud.

Up and downward moved the light,
Beckoning now where sands gleam white—
Now upon Carn Barra height .—
    " Well done, Meraud ! "

Broke the slow dawn, pale and grey—
Down beside Carn Barra Bay,
On the shore, they sought the prey—
    Not Meraud.

Something lay upon the sand :
Slow and weary down the strand,
The spent lantern in her hand,
    Came Meraud.

And she saw the dead man lie,
With his still face to the sky ;—
And one bitter, piercing cry
    Gave Meraud.

By his side her father knelt,
Searching vest and pouch and belt ;—
Pity she had never felt
    Thrilled Meraud,

For the young face, once so fair,—
With the curls of soft, dark hair,—
Bruised and marred, and past all care
    Of Meraud.

On them all in their surprise
Flamed the light of wrathful eyes—
"You shall leave him where he lies !"
    Cried Meraud.

And she kissed him as he lay,—
Washed off the salt sand and spray :—
So beside him all the day
    Sat Meraud.

In her arms she held him still
Through the short day dark and chill.
"Nevermore I'll do your will !"
    Said Meraud.

Then they gave him Christian grace,
Bore him to the holy place,
Dumb for awe of that white face
    Of Meraud.

Laid him on St. Levan's height,
Where the spray drives blinding white,
Of a howling winter's night—
                    O Meraud !

Night by night she crept up there
To the graveyard bleak and bare,
Like a ghost with long black hair,
                    Pale Meraud.

When the sky the lightnings clave,
When the wildest storm-winds drave,
On her face across the grave
                    Lay Meraud.

In the dawning wild and wan
They found her, when the year began   .
So for love of that dead man
                    Died Meraud.

BEATRIX.

B RIGHT was the glow on sky and earth,
   And her heart was light and her face was fair ;—
Rich gifts God gave her at her birth,
   And hearts grew glad for the love of her.

And fair thoughts nested 'neath her gold hair,
   And her heart was a bower of singing birds,
And her eyes were aglow with the music there,
   Till it trembled over her lips into words.

And a white, white bird with a crimson breast
   Was ever the bird that sang most sweet,—
Within her heart he had built his nest,
   And his song was the pulse that made it beat.

She heard and felt,—and it brought the glow
   Into her cheek, she knew not why ;—
But she loved all creatures more, I know,
   And was all the fairer to mortal eye.

And then she awoke, and was ware of it,
   And knew whence came the light of her day.
And she said to herself, " It is not fit."
   And she frayed the Bird of Love away.

But the old songs came to her lips no more,
   And the old light came no more to her eyes ;—
The birds were dumb that had sung before,—
   They fly with the scornèd Love when he· flies.

And at greatest need failed strength and pride,—
   She sank down weeping in weary pain,
And, helpless and humbled, vainly cried
   For the Bird of Love to come again.

HERAKLEITOS.

SADLY he of Ephesus
  Looked upon the world,
Standing on the rocky beach
  Where the white waves curled,—

Saw the great tides ebb and flow,
  Moon and stars arise,
Blackness cover that red rock
  Where the sunset lies ;—

Saw the green leaves spring and fade,
  Saw bright eyes grow dim,
And the bounding life die out
  Slow from heart and limb.

Nothing ever stays the same,—
  Whether joy or woe :
He took his book, and sadly wrote ;
  " *All things ebb and flow.*"

Madly in this dizzy whirl
  All things spin and spin ;—
Herakleitos asked himself,
  " How did it begin ? "

"Is it well?" again he asked,
    "This unresting change?—
Shall it be for evermore
    Still as sad and strange?"

Ask he might, but answer none,
    For his heart arose ;—
Weary down he laid himself :—
Now, I think, he knows.

—

THE ENCHANTED GARDEN.

DOWN in Naples, legends tell us, long ago,
    Virgil had a garden on Mount Posilipo.

Virgil, the sweet singer with the mournful eyes,—
Virgil, the enchanter, great and wondrous wise.

On that laughing headland 'mid the summer seas
Set his magic garden of herbs and incense-trees.

Blood-red rose, and moonlight lily, and the red
Heavy-scented poppies we strew above the dead,—

Amaranthus, growing on Elysian leas,
And the golden apples of th' Hesperides,—

All of these,—and flowers for which no mortal hath a
    name ;—
Oh ! the shifting splendours of rainbow-tinted flame !

And within that garden grew a herb apart,
A herb to heal all sickness and pain and sorrow of
    heart,—

With a starry blossom white as driven snow,
And "*Herb-Lucius*" Virgil named it, long ago.

Ever bloomed that garden, fed with gentle dew—
Summer never parched it, winter never slew ;

Nor the fierce Sirocco, when, in his heat and glare,
Blighting, blasting, burning, he fell on earth and air.

Girt in robe wide-flowing, when the eve was still,
Walked the Master in his garden on the hill.

Lips a-thrill with music that his spirit hears—
Eyes aglow with quiet joy, yet dim with mist of tears.

Blue are still the waters,—green is Cumae's shore,—
But the magic garden find we nevermore.

Gone the herb of healing—and we watch in vain
For the gentle Mage to walk amid his flowers again.

THE MERMAID OF ZENNOR.

DOWN by Zennor the waves were white
With the western gale that had blown all night.

Heaped on the sand as the tide went down
Were the wreaths of tangle and oar-weed brown.

Penwith of Penwith stood on the strand—
Red broke the dawn on the Cornish land.

White and golden out there in the bay—
What lies on the reef where the breakers play ?

It is not the foam of the surges white
Nor the brown sea-tangle that ripples so bright.

The sun on the water flashed crimsonly—
It blinded his eyes that he could not see.

But it seemed to him that he could hear
A wild voice ringing out sweet and clear.

A woman's voice o'er the sunlit sea,—
And all that she sang was "Come to me !"

Penwith of Penwith stood on the strand,
The comeliest lad in the Cornish land,—

F

And but for a moment he was ware
Of a white, white woman with golden hair,

And laughing lips, and eyes that could win
Men's souls from them, for the sweetness therein.

" Come," she sang, and beckoned to greet :—
The foam was hissing about his feet —

First to ankle, and then to knee,
Deeper and deeper into the sea.

And her eyes, and her voice, and her long hair's flow,
They drew him, and would not let him go,

Away and away from Zennor shore;—
And Penwith of Penwith came back no more.

THE LAST OF THE REAPERS.

O H ! ho ! ho ! midnight is soon,—
High in heaven the harvest moon,—
And the stars, like maidens all in white
Pass through the blue vault of the night :—
And the sea-beach glitters with white-fringed foam,—
Oh ! ho ho ! for the harvest home.

Oh ! ho, ho ! for the harvest home !
Oh ! what a night afar to roam !
Sing ! is it not enough of bliss
To be on earth such a night as this ?
Light, maybe is the sheaf I bring,—
But there was the joy of gathering !

Hark !—the crash,—and the long, low roar,
Rattle and hiss on the pebbly shore—
Outside the sea lies silvered and still,
And the white moon leads it as she will,
But over the rocks flies the leaping foam—
Oh ! ho, ho ! for the harvest home !

Bare and white does the braeside lie,
Harvested clean beneath the sky :—
Stubbles are sharp to the barefoot tread,—
It seems the others are far ahead ;—
Never mind me—I come ! I come !
Oh ! ho ho ! for the harvest home !

Surely there grows a chill in the air . . . .
What was that ghostly cry out there?—
Only the lapwings!—and far away
The startled curlew pipe in the bay—
A chill in the sky, and a cloud on the moon—
Methinks it is time for her setting soon.

Oh! ho ho! for the harvest home!
Dry in the cup is the red wine's foam,
And the lamps are out, and the feast is done,—
And I meet the people, one by one,
Coming out to their work—and lo!—
I turn—in the East the sunrise-glow.

A REVERIE.

OH! bring me poppies!
  Poppies are for sleep!
Poppies hath Persephone
 In her palace deep.
She holds them in her hands,
 And she wreathes them in her hair,—
In the blue-black waves of night,—
 That pale Queen sad and fair. . .
They are crimson, but not like blood,—
 They glow like coals of fire,—
  Oh! Queen Persephone,
   Grant me my desire!

Bring me, bring me poppies,
 That last never a day!
They wilt and drop within the hour,—
 But oh! there's not a fairer flower
In summer's bright array.
 Poppies are for sleep,
And poppies are for death ;—
 And for the glowing lips
That breathe a short life's breath.
 They last not a day,
  But oh! so fair, so fair!
 Oh! Queen Persephone,
  Braid them in thy hair!—

Crimson, goodliest crimson,—
  Glowing through and through
With a black spot at the heart,—
  Heavy with morning dew ;—
Black, black at the heart,
  That is for death—
Death, and the shadows
  In the realms beneath ;—
Crimson—that's for joy of life
  And the summer sun,—
That is why she loves them,
  Whose joy of life is done !
And when the shadows gather,
  And life's woe grows too deep,
Then Queen Persephone
  Kisses us to sleep ;
She strews the poppies round us
  And shrouds us in her hair,
And kisses us, and kisses us
  Out of our despair.
Then bring me the poppies
  That are so rich and fair,
And such as Queen Persephone
  Has wreathèd in her hair !
Poppies are for sleep —
  And sleep is like to death,
And I'm aweary, weary,
And it has grown a burden
  To draw this mortal breath.

      Strew them all around me,
        Crimson, glowing deep,—
      Give me one in my right hand,
        And let me sleep.

WINDOW-PANE RECORDS.

" J. McNeill, from Colonsay, Argyleshire, 1807-8-9."

SECOND floor, and left-hand window,
　　Top-sash, in the corner pane,
You can see a diamond-graven
　　Scrawl of an inscription plain.
Eighteen hundred—seven, is it?—
　　Oh ! what years have passed away,
Since the man who owned this chamber
　　Was McNeill of Colonsay !

Who were you ? A student, clearly,
　　Come to take your three years' grind ;
Did you fancy mathematics ?
　　And was Logic to your mind ?
Or did these old walls re-echo,
　　'Mid the clink of glasses gay,
Gaelic toasts, " with all the honours,"
　　To McNeill of Colonsay ?

What's become of you, I wonder ?
　　Does this planet hold you still ?
Are you sleeping with your fathers
　　On some windy, cairn-topped hill ?
Or might some far Highland parish
　　In the mist-wrapped islands grey,
Know you yet, and own your labours,
　　O McNeill of Colonsay ?

Oh ! my ghostly predecessor,
   Do I see you seated there,
Reading by the flickering fire-light
   Plato in my great arm-chair ?
With the thoughtful Scottish forehead,
   And the deep eyes' changeful play,
Grim lips curved to tender fancies,—
   John McNeill of Colonsay !

Seems to me I feel your presence
   Evermore about the room,
When the winter nights are eerie,
   And I'm lonely in the gloom.
Were you ever homesick, longing
   For the drifting of the spray,
When the billows break on Jura,—
   John McNeill of Colonsay ?

See I'm sitting by the fireside ;
   Come and take the other chair !
Tired, I'd like a chat this evening,
   Work not done—I do not care !
Come and tell me in the firelight
   What you did here in your day,—
What you think about the Phaedo,
   John McNeill of Colonsay !

St. Andrew's March, 1885.

—

NYMPHOLEPTOS.

IT was in the forest-deeps,
   Where the beeches are green on high,
And the golden sunshine sleeps,
   Shut out from the blue of the sky,
And the mountain-brook down-leaps,
That he saw the Vision, which steeps
   Men's souls in fire, till they follow—
   And he who follows, must die.

Only once—and the gleam of her eyes
   Hath kindled a light in his soul
More than of moons that rise,
   More than of stars that roll ;
And the brow so holy and wise,
And the lips where locked sweetness lies . .
   And he must follow, follow,
   Though he never reach the goal.

He sprang through the tangled brake—
   He tore his hands on the thorn,
He splashed through the reeds of the lake,
   And the black night passed, and the morn
Reddened, and found him awake,—
And the lynx, and the water-snake
   Stirred, starting at him who followed
   The trail, all weary and worn.

Where the slopes are mossy and green,—
　Where the laurels bloom in the shade,—
He waited with reverent mien,
　When the noon-glory flooded the glade,
He knelt, and waited his queen,
To catch but her garment's sheen
　　He strained his eyes in the twilight,
　　And watched—and was not afraid.

When the hemlocks were black in the sky,
　And the stars looked down on his doom,
He followed their course on high,
　And he heard the bittern boom—
For he wandered far and nigh,
Wherever the night-owls cry,
　　And the glowing eyes of the panther
　　Gleam green through the forest gloom.

And changed and marred of face,
　He came back to the dwellings of men:—
They knew not of the grace
　That had come to him there and then
In the lonely forest-place,—
So they pitied his bitter case,
　　Or laughed, maybe—and he left them,
　　To follow the track again.

And under the wide blue heaven,
  On a bare and lone hill-side
Of splintered granite, storm-riven,
  They found him, with arms flung wide,
As if he had vainly striven,
Desperate and frenzy-driven
  To clasp the feet of his Vision,
  That flashed on his sight as he died.

BY THE ROADSIDE.

April 5th, 1883.

A HAGGARD woman, pale and plain,
  In a commonplace, every-day bonnet and shawl—
Such as you meet again and again ;—
  Forty or thereabouts, thin and tall,
  With the flattest of prose for her life—that's all.

Now, on this sweetest of April days,
  When the bitter east winds have ceased to blow,
When the hills are softened in tender haze.—
  What should she be doing, I'd like to know,
  By the gate of the wood where the primroses grow ?

She stood on the road and leaned on the gate,
  With dim eyes fixed on the springing green,—
The flowers that come, and the leaves that wait ;
  Even as a young maid might stand and lean,
  And wait for the love as yet unseen.

And she held in her hand—O my heart, was it so ?—
  Rushes that grow by the roadside ditch,
Seven or so—the old trick do you know ?
  Knot the ends together—you don't see which,
  And mark if the ring comes without a hitch.

If the ends are joined to make one wide ring,
   Good is your lot : so the old saws go ;—
If you open your hand, and find the thing
   Twofold or threefold, that is woe.
   Was she trying her future so ?—

Not much future, you'd think, she had . . . .
   Or rather—an idle trick you try
In those dreamy moments, half-sad, half-glad,
   When the salt mist comes up and dims your eye,
   As you rock on the waves of the days gone by.

So the soft, sweet airs, and the smile of old earth,
   Struck home to the heart of her who stood,
In the midst of her sad life's barren dearth,
   Lingering by the primrose-wood,
   And she vaguely felt, " After all, it is good.—"

MURIEL.

'TWAS in the July morning,
    When I had crossed the stile,
I met her coming down the path,
    And singing all the while.

She had been seeking early,
    In the golden fields at morn
The fairest of the poppies,
    And the ripest of the corn.

There was light in the dewy grass,
    There was light in the sunbeam's birth,—
But into her face was gathered
    The light of heaven and earth.

And on she passed through the meadows,
    With step so light and fleet,
With the dark, dark curls about her brow,
    And the dews about her feet.

So we passed each other that morning,
    And nothing did we say,—
But a sunbeam fell upon my heart,
    And lay there all the day.

MY SHIP.

MY ship!—my ship!—she waits for me,
Rocking in some green western bay.
The white waves laugh upon the sea,
  Afar the ripples hiss and play
Along the bright sands in their glee.

Far in the blue the heron cries,
  The oak-wood whispers green and cool,—
Swinging at anchor there she lies,
  My ship—my own, my beautiful !
And all things love her—earth and skies.

All things do love her—seas and skies :
  The white clouds stoop as they would kiss ;
The merry wind that singing flies,
  He knows no fairer thing than this—
Nor the sweet birds that are so wise.

The ripples break against her side ;—
  Her white sails dazzle in the blue,—
The woods dream, mirrored in the tide,—
  She, slowly swinging, dreameth too   .   .   .
But when I heard the west wind glide

Amid the pines upon the hill,
  Just now, she leapt and strained her bands,
Panting alive with quivering will.
  When will they rise—those strange new lands ?—
I come—I come—my own ! be still !

She wakes !—she calls !—How long ? How long ?--
   The anchor-cable heaves and strains,--
And Life is leaping, young and strong,
   With spring-fire flushing in her veins,
A-dream with colour, light, and song.

My ship—my ship !—she waits for me !—
   And all the world is fresh and fair :—
The blessed spring-time's mystery
   Has washed it clean of fear and care ;—
Life pulses fast by land and sea.

Away ! away !—the sunrise-glow
   Burns on the waves : O joy of life !—
O new wine, strong in sparkling flow,
   God pours us forth ! O bliss of strife !—
At last !—at last !—and Westward ho !—

IN A THEATRE.

Capua, 72 B.C.

WE were friends and comrades loyal though I was
of alien race,
And he a free-born Samnite that followed the man
from Thrace,
And there, in the mid-arena, he and I stood face to face.

I was a branded swordsman, and he was supple and
strong.
They saved us alive from the battle, to do us this
cruellest wrong,
That each should slay the other there before the staring
throng.

Faces—faces—and faces ! how it made my brain to spin !
Beautiful faces of women, and tiger-souls therein !
And merry voices of girls that laughed, debating of who
should win.

Over us, burning and cloudless, dazzled the blue sky's
dome ;
Far away to the eastward the white snow-peaks of his
home ;
And in front the Prefect, purple-clad, in the deadly
might of Rome.

G

And so, in the mid-arena, we stood there face to face,
And he looked me right in the eyes and said, "I ask
  thee one last grace—
Slay me, for *thee* I cannot." Then I held his hand a
  space,

But knew not what I answered: the heavens round
  and wide
Surged up and down—a flash of steel—my sword was
  through his side,
And I was down upon my knees, and held him as he
  died.

His blood was warm on my fingers, his eyes were scarcely
  still,
When they tore him from me, and the blade that else
  had healed all ill.
And it is one more day I am theirs, to work their will.

No matter! the sand, and the sun, and the faces hateful
  to see,
They will be nothing—nothing! but I wonder who
  may be
The other man I have to fight—the man that shall
  kill me!

TOWAN CROSS, CORNWALL.

O GREEN earth, let me love thee! How at times
   We fain would break away from cares that hold,—
From this our daily life's unvarying mould,
And find us, face to face, in other climes,
With thee—but free from work-dust that begrimes
   Our face, and blinds our vision,—manifold
   Wonders of thine, outstretched upon the wold,
Beholding,—listening to the deep sea's chimes.

A lonely glen beside the western sea
   I know, deep-cleft between the granite hills,
   Where heather-bells ring peace into the soul,
And the west wind is like a kiss to me ;—
   To lie upon that turf, and hear the rills,
   When I am sick of heart, would make me whole.

SUNDAY MORNING.

Cambridge.

THE sunshine sleeps upon the market-square,—
   The gray stone fountain in the quietness
   Ripples with gentle murmur, that the press
Of feet and din of voices overbear
On week-days ;—o'er the flagstones, here and there
   Trip rainbow-breasted doves ; and May's caress
   Lingers on square tower, fretted pinnacles,
Blue skies, green elms, and all things that are fair.
And God seems near—the God our souls adore.—
And that dark phantom the world bends before
   Bidding us name it thus, shrinks back forlorn ;
And, as the restful glory wraps us round,
St. Mary's bells, a crystal rain of sound
   Break on the clearness of the golden morn.

SONG.

A STRANGE wild noon of storm and shine,—
The south wind's balm like spicy wine,
I wandered forth when the rain was done,
And the flowers I brought, I brought for one.

The golden, great marsh-marigolds,
And purple plumes the sedge-bank holds,
And milky stitchwort from the lanes,
And blue-bells wet with sweet May rains.

And all the glories of the May
Were round me as I passed to-day :—
The rains unlocked the lap of earth
Whence love and sweetness have their birth.

And crystal drops on all the leaves,—
And grass in diamond-studded sheaves,
And springing buds, and birds that wake
To music for the sweet spring's sake.

So, both hands full I bring to you .   .   .   .
. . Nay, heed not that, the brambles grew
Beside the flowers,—and thorns can tear—
I have the flowers, that's all I care.

SONNET.

O BLUE sea, once I thought death were no pain,
Rocked in thine arms unto our last long sleep,—
And sweet the death-dirge of the waves that weep
Along the weed-fringed shore, and I were fain
To lie upon thy breast, nor wake again,—
O great, beloved, cruel-hearted deep!—
But when I felt the waters round me sweep,
Half-stunned and blinded, struggling all in vain,—
O then I felt the horror that it is
To stand by death and look him in the face,—
A helpless thing, betwixt the sea and sky,
And hear his low voice in the ripple hiss—
No soul to see or save in that lone place ;—
And cried to God in anguish not to die.

ELIPHAZ THE TEMANITE.

" Consolatores onerosi omnes vos estis."

I KNOW not what you say to me,
  Your words fall dead upon my ears :
Surely the same our hopes and fears
And that for which we strive, should be.

And yet—and yet—Oh ! nought but strife
  And bitterness can come of this ;
  Leave me alone where silence is,
Leave me alone with God my life.

I do not doubt—I am not vexed,
  By heart-sick strivings vainly tost,—
  I've found what never can be lost,
Though weary oft and sore perplexed

By what I see in this poor world ;
  Yet God doth triumph at the last :
  Upon this rock my feet stand fast,
Wherefrom I never can be hurled.

I do not want your comfortings,
  I do not want to strive with you ;
  But side by side to dare and do,
As God gives,—each in different things.

I know that all things right shall be,
  Yet nought can say my faith to prove,—
  I rest upon the Eternal Love—
Leave us alone, my God and me.

VICTORIA CITY.*

BACK again my spirit yearns,
　　From the roaring of the street,
From the city's heart that burns,
　　Throbbing in its fevered heat
To the hemlock's swaying, and the wild wind's playing,
　　And the creek that rushes at my feet.

To the mountains, forest-clad,
　　To the maple's rosy blush,
Where the robins whistle glad,
　　And the blue-jay through the bush
Flashes like the glory of a fairy story,
　　And my footsteps echo in the hush.

To the old birch by the creek
　　Where the shade was black at noon,
And the hill we used to seek
　　With its cool spring's silver boon,
Or the grassy glade, where they in the shade
　　Waited for the deer beneath the moon.

Oh ! the crystal autumn days
　　When the sunflowers blossomed wide,—
Thousand golden suns ablaze
　　Over every green hill side !
Oh ! the saw-mill's steam, that with a rainbow-gleam
　　Sprang into the sunlight, and then died !—

* Potter Co. Pa. U.S.A.

Three log shanties, and a mill,
   And a house that was to be
Stood for all our city :—nil
   It remained by Fate's decree ;
No new walls arose, when that winter's snows
   Covered all the hemlocks silently.

Nothing ever but a name
   Our " Victoria City " there
By the Cross Fork Creek became :—
   Failure—and almost despair ;—
And the snows came down, and the maples brown
   Moan ed out lonely on the bitter air.

How is it by Cross Fork Creek
   After all the years have been ?
Has some other come to seek
   Better fortune there, and seen
Life's full-flowing tide from the old world wide,
   Rush into the solemn stillness green ?

Have they cut the hemlocks down—
   Those we left—and burnt the brush ?
Have they from Germania town
   Brought a railroad ?   Has the crush
Of the haggard crowd with their murmur loud
   Broken sharply in upon the hush ?

Better so I know it is—
  I mourn not for days of yore,—
But I like to think of this,
  Somehow, as it was before,
When the trees were glowing, and the creek clear-flowing,
  In the childhood-days that are no more.

Blessings on it !—whatsoe'er
  May have come to it since then—
May God keep it fresh and fair—
  Busy, happy home of men ! —
In the old-world city, full of woe and pity,
  Oh ! how I have longed to see it once again !—

QUEEN CIRCE.

I WAS a Chian sailor-lad,
 The gayest of them all—
Till the day she made of me
 The dog before the hall.
And I lie on the doorstep,
 And watch night and day,
And man or beast that likes her not,
 I scare them all away.

We came to her castle,
 That summer's day so fine,
And there she set before us
 The meat and the wine :
Men of Crete and Samos,
 And the golden Cyclades,—
And she smiled, and bade us rest our souls
 From perils of the seas.

Oh ! so tall and beautiful
 In her flowing purple gown
And in her hair a golden snake
 Was twisted for a crown :—
And her eyes like stars in the heaven,
 And her lips, they were so red,—
And I looked on her, and touched not
 The wine nor the bread.

They laughed and they shouted
  As they drank of her wine,—
She changed them all to oxen—
  To asses and to swine ;—
She gave me the cup,
  And I drank, and knew no more, —
And now I am the watch-dog
  That lies before the door.

She passes in and out
  As I watch before the door,—
And I listen, listen for the beat
  Of her sandals on the floor.
My life long I'm enchanted,
  Her slave for to be—
But who would not ?—O ! who would not,
  For such a witch as she ?

ARGEMONE.

O NCE, when the summer burned upon the land,
I went forth while the eastern sun was low,
To watch the ripples in their murmuring flow,
Lifting the wreaths of weed upon the sand.
All else was shut from sight but sea and strand
By the low grass-grown ridge, that holds the woe
Of waters from the fields, when fierce winds blow.
The silent sweep of shore on either hand
Brightened with morning: silver cloud-flecks passed
Across the pale blue, with the wind that rose,—
As, over shingle, sand, and turfy lea,
I wandered on, and found the spot at last,
Where 'mid grey leaves in mystic glory glows
The strange, lone, golden flower that loves the sea.

· MISERERE.

PITY me, O ye careless ones that pass
 With dancing footsteps through the dewy grass,—
Me who beside your pathway sit alone,
A worthless, broken life, and make my moan,—
     Oh, pity me!

Pity me, thou, O world that passest by,
With crowned, averted head and scornful eye,—
Thy bitter blame strikes sharp ; yet even thou,
If that thou knewest, would'st have compassion now,—
     Oh, pity me!

Pity me, ye whose hearts are yet unvext
By life's hard problems,—me who sore perplext,
Sit in thick darkness, straining weary eyes
Vainly—for whom no moon nor star doth rise :
     Oh, pity me!

Pity me, strong ones with the steadfast brows,
Whose steps are straight towards your father's house,
Who bravely think, nor fear to speak your thought,—
Me, coward, in mine own heart's toils fast caught,—
     Oh, pity me!

Pity me, too, ye strong and reckless-hearted,
From whom all clogging tremor has departed,
Who fearless sin, and laughing set your lips
To the sweet, wild cup that shall your souls eclipse,—
     Oh, pity me!

Pity me, O my God!   Dost thou not know
The fierce dark storms that rend man's spirit so,
Vain longings—dumb perplexities?   Thy Name
Is love, they said.   Thou'rt evermore the same!
                              Oh, pity me!

My God!—and if I am a failure, bruised,
And worthless.   Thou, who madest, hast refused,
And cast me off?   Thou canst not!   Since Thou art,
All's well—and why should I ask any heart
                              To pity me?

NOT THERE.

NOT there—not there—and all the feast is turned
To gall !
Not there !—the lights and music throbbed and burned
Athwart the hall—
But darkness fell upon my soul that yearned,
And discord—like a pall.

Not there ! and what are sky and earth this morn
To me ?—
The rippling river, and the standing corn
So fair to see ?—
When all of beauty that was ever born
Is but a frame to thee !

Not there !—and in the holy house my knees
I bow !—
I thought one face would help the love and peace
In praise and vow :—
But all I am is out of tune with these—
O God !—forgive me now !—

RALSTON.

San Francisco, 1872.

WHAT were his thoughts as he went that day,
   With the swinging step and the quiet eye,
Down to Potrero by the bay—
   Down to the shore at noon to die?

Not a man to pity, maybe,—
   Not a life that you'd think so fair ;—
Not a tragedy hero he,
   This California millionaire.

He'd played with his thousands as they were dust—
   He'd staked and won, and had had his fling ;—
And the end had come, as ever it must,
   And this was his day of reckoning.

He stepped to the Bank that day from his house,—
   Handed in his resignation they say,—
And crushed his hat down over his brows,
   And then he went down to the baths in the Bay.

A strong, bold man, and he loved the sea,—
   And the salt spray would cool his weary brain—
So they said who watched him—but he
   Never swam to the shore again.

II

Cowardice?—maybe—but who shall dare
  To track the way that his wild thoughts ran?
Was it the pride that could not bear
  To face the world as a ruined man?

Or was it that, in his bitter shame
  For the good he'd meant, and the ill he'd done,
He would be beforehand with this world's blame,
  Nor longer live in the face of the sun?

Was it . . . . ?   He's past our wonderings:
  Needs not *our* verdict on either side   .   .   .   .
Wonder what now he thinks of these things,
  Lying so still in the wash of the tide?

EAST WINDS IN MARCH.

L ANGUID weeks crept slowly on—
Spring not come, nor winter gone
Chill grey skies, and mist and rain,
Sickening cares and bright hopes slain :
When will Summer come again ?

Out of the East leapt the wind of the Lord,
Clear and keen as the Archangel's sword,—
Cleft a blue rift in the cloudy grey,
Chased the rank mist from the meads away—
Whitened the westward seas with spray.

And there broke a voice from the waiting earth,—
No voice of joy or the summer's mirth :
No ripple of laughing, springtide song—
But a clarion-cry, out-shrilling strong,
Of one that has been at ease too long.

Welcome, welcome, to pain and strife !
We will none of the life that is not life !
Earth is aweary and sore forlorn :
Give us the agony whence is born
The victory-joy of the summer morn.

THE GREAT REVEALER.

NOTHING real but Death? . . .
 And death is real—*real* you say?
And *I* shall know it one day?
How the thought halloweth!
I, even I, with these hands and feet,
And eyes that look on the clear sunshine,—
I, even I, with this heart and brain
Shall look on that thing, so dread, so sweet!—
I, with this common life of mine—
Failures again and yet again—
That I should enter in
After all folly and sin
Into the holiest shrine!
Oh! I scarce can believe it true—
True and certain for me and you!
Really to feel the pulses cease
That oft in the temples throb and ache,
And all wild longings melt into peace ;—
To lie down to a sweet, sweet sleep
And be in the other world when you wake ;
In that unseen world that is round us and near,
Only we cannot see it or hear :—
To have slipt off the flesh with its gateways of sense,
And to *know*, with no seeing or hearing between—
That were strange, and wondrous, I ween . .

And this is certain,—without pretence ?—
And—just a slip of your feet—
Or the miss of one single heart-beat—
Or a beautiful steel-blade bright,
Driven home by an enemy's hand—
And you might know it to-night !

O Death ! thou art wise ! thou art kind !
There is no teacher like thee !
All thou wilt tell us, that the mind,
Here in its prison-bars confined,
Beats out its life and can never see.
And I, even I, who have not lived
Worthily of so great a boon
Shall hear the silver spheres in tune—
The harmony of the Universe,—
And know that Being is not a curse,
                    Soon—yes, soon !
And all that perplexes me here
Will never be worth a tear,
For I shall see, with heart set free,
The tides that come and go
And rock the great world to and fro,—
And the great eternal Law
That rules them all ; and know
It is well for the race of men
That breathe the upper air,
And well for those who have passed
We know not where.
Oh ! the bliss and the awe

Of the plunge in the unknown sea
Of what is yet to be!
O Death!—Oh! surely the glory
Is more than I can bear!—
And what are a few little years,
Even though dark, and wet with tears,
If thou art all this to me?

"DENVER, COLORADO."

" Cœlum, non animum mutant, qui trans mare currunt."

L IFE somehow seems to creep slowly here—
Too sad for a smile, not worth a tear ;
The brightness of all things has died away,
The freshness of hope in the early day,—
Yet still in one's ear there rings along
The burden of some outlandish song
     Of " Denver, Colorado."

What should it mean ? and why is this ?—
No fabled haven of Eden-bliss,
No Eldorado of childish dreams,
Or gorgeous visions by Eastern streams
Of palms and temples with gold aflame—
Yet there's some vague charm in the very name
     Of " Denver, Colorado."

In the fair dream-pictures of long ago,
When young hearts yearned to the sunset glow,
And the wondrous West where the world is young,
It caught one's ear, and it slips to one's tongue,
When the longings come up from time to time
For a freer life, and a fresher clime,
     And " Denver, Colorado."

When life seems a failure, blank and bare,
And sweet ideals have vanished in air,
And work is undone that I had to do,
And the power to do it seems going too—
It's Oh ! and it's Oh ! but I were fain
To start afresh, and begin again,
                    In " Denver, Colorado."

One's sick of self and all its ill,
And the thousand small falsehoods that creep and kill ?
One feels as if, once set face to face
With the facts of life, and given the grace
To suffer and do, from conventions free,
One could build up a new life worthily,
                    In "Denver, Colorado."

But alas ! and alas ! the fancy's vain—
I'm longing to look on the West again,
While *here* is the battle to fight and win :
I blame the world—but the fault's within.
I should only meet with myself once more,
And maybe a hatefuller self than before,
                    In " Denver, Colorado."

IN THE GULF OF MEXICO.

GREY cloud-curtains half withdrawn :—
Moaning seas, at break of dawn,
    Heave and swell
On the desolate sand, wreck-strawn—
    Ysabel !

Where the mountain, silver bright,—
Looks afar upon the white
    Citadel :
Where the plague and tempest fight,—
    Ysabel !

Far beyond the dreary town,
Where the level sands slope down, —
    Mark it well,
White upon the bare sands brown—
    Ysabel !

Swooping birds with cruel cries,—
Bitter wrath of seas and skies
    Her death-knell,—
Look where a drowned woman lies—
    Ysabel !

White limbs bruised and battered sore,
As the surf upon the shore
    Rose and fell,—
Eyes that lighten nevermore—
    Ysabel !

Eyes of might for bale or bliss
Darkened in a trance like this—
 Lost their spell ;—
Lips that never man may kiss,—
 Ysabel!

Washing wild the loose, dark hair—
Hands outstretched—in one last prayer ?—
 Who can tell ?
Was there none to save thee there,—
 Ysabel!

Sweep her back, O cruel sea !
In thy great arms tenderly
 Fold her well :—
Fairest, sweetest slain by thee,—
 Ysabel!

—

LEAINA.

WHAT name had she ;—what soft Greek syllables
Melted upon his lips, who murmured them
Into her ear 'twixt kiss and kiss ? . . No name
Is hers to us but that : *The Lioness*,
The which they graved in stone Pentelican,
And set on high in Athens for all time.

She was a dark-tressed girl, with laughing lips,—
Of sweet Miletus, not Athenian born—
Or she had never had such supple grace
Of rounded limb, or tender curve of cheek,
Ripened in Asian sunlight,—or such slow
Dark languorous eyes, where lightnings lay asleep. .
And she could sing like summer nightingales
When mid-May moons are white ;—and when she spake,
Her voice was soft-caressing as a dove's,
With a little rippling plash of laughter in't,
Like to the summer wave upon the sand.

And you would think this woman solely made
To love and be loved, as Greeks counted love
Mostly in sunny Hellas ; without too much
Of love's sweet patience or love's constancy,—
To love, without love's pain, a summer long ;—
And then——Where are the butterflies, in times
Of autumn-winds and snow ? . . . .
                    Well, so one thought .
And yet this woman loved——as *we* count love

Maybe she was a laughing, soulless thing,
While her love's summer lasted,—thinking most
Of the white roses twined amid her braids
Of shining purple-black, and how those red
Twin armlets of the tawny Persian gold,
With rubies in their serpent-heads for eyes,
Burned on the smooth, pale, olive skin, and broke
The sweeping curve of shapely arm . . . Or, no :
Not quite—for, as those sweet weeks passed, it fell
She thought of one who gave the armlets too ;
And under all her smiles, and ringing laugh,
And merry mischief, and gay dalliance with
One and another—each as good as all,
Lay one thought sleeping, growing in his sleep .—
The unperceived grave Love, with solemn brow,
And set lips, and sword girt upon his thigh.

And she knew not—nor any—till that Love woke.

The waking was upon this wise.   There fell
A tumult in the city,—men had sworn
To slay the tyrant ;—and one tried, and failed,
And he was slain ; — and thereupon they sought
All who had helped or known of it—and lo !
The man this alien woman loved was one.

She knew it—she had heard them talk of it
That summer evening at the feast ; when he,
Resting his sunny curls against her knees,
Sang softly of the sword and myrtle-boughs ;—
And his grey eyes grew wide, and glowed with light,
Looking upon Aristogeiton's face,

Who stood up calm beside his own heart's friend,
And swore—his right hand lifted up, the left'
On that friend's shoulder laid,—to do or die . . .
She knew it all,—and how, when morning came,
He laughed it off as 'twere an idle dream,
And diced, and drank, and sang, and kissed again ;—
And so the days sped softly . . . till he saw
Upon the Agora the lifted spears,
And young Harmodios in his beauty laid
Dead at his feet who would have died for him,—
And shuddered, for he knew his turn might come.

And then the sleeping Love awoke in her,
All stern and grand as he of Ephesus,—
And lifted up his sword, and smote her soul.
And, sick at heart, she tried to smile and sing,
As heretofore, and not to shiver when
A step came near, or any stranger spake
With her beloved,—laughing when he said,
" *Aedonion, my little nightingale,*
Why lookest thou so pale ?"—And then by night
She slept not, sobbing out her pain alone.

Three days—and then before the tyrant's seat
They haled her—asked her many things,—but she,
Heart all a-flutter like a netted bird,
Would answer nought for fear of saying all.
She knew not what would come,—she only knew
His life was in her hand,—and she must die
Before she spoke. No more. She had no high
Heroic resolution, said no fierce

Wild words defying tyrants ; . . . but, when she saw
The racks and scorpion-whip, went white as death,—
Gave one look round with great bewildered eyes,
And slim, soft fingers locked ;—and when one tore
The shawl from those white shoulders, seized, and thrust
Her towards that thing, she gave a piteous scream,
And hid her face.—How could she bear it ? how ?
She who had never felt the touch of pain
Worse than a rose-thorn's prick . . . Oh ! what
    to do ?
And those fierce faces pitiless all around . . .
And none could help in all the world save he
Who could not—must not . . . Surely . . .
    would she not
Shriek out his name in spite of all, when once
That iron claspt her wrist ? Oh !—but to die
She had thought death was such a dreadful thing—
Quickly, and have it o'er !——

                    So when they laid
Her on the rack, and quick, fierce flying gasps
Of anguish shook the little, panting breast,
Such fear had she of speaking in the trance
Of pain, that name, that—one last effort more,
And she had bitten through the tongue that spake
Such tender words, but yesterday . . . and then,
When she had put all speech beyond her power,
The close-prest lips and set teeth parting wide,
One terrible, inarticulate cry brake forth,
Not to be held in ; then the agony
Of wrenching joints and muscles strained, wrung out

Wail upon wail—yet still no sign—low moans
Fainter and fainter growing. till her eyes,
Wide, blind, and staring. opened on the sky,
And the fierce sun-blaze could not hurt them more.

And so that alien woman loved and died,—
And none in after years can know her name :
That died with her—the stained and scorned name
Men knew her by in Athens :—she shall be
Remembered as Leaina evermore,
Who truly loved and bravely died for love.

THE UPAS-TREE.

THERE fell a seed of the Upas-tree,
 I know not whence it came to me,
I know not how or when it fell,
But I marked the spot and I loved it well,
 The young, green shoot of the Upas-tree.

It grew and spread—the Upas-tree,
Its leaves were comely and fair to see,
And the lithe brown boughs like snakes to behold,.
And the fruit was apples of burning gold ;
 And my heart was glad of the Upas-tree.

My heart was mad for the Upas-tree,
I loved and cherished it jealously ;
Nought had I loved so through all the years,
With burning heart's blood and bitter tears,
 I watered the roots of my Upas-tree.

My heart was mad for the Upas-tree,—
It knew nought else upon earth or sea :
Against its trunk I laid my breast,
And my arms clung round it as to their rest,—
 O my beautiful Upas-tree !

O my beautiful Upas-tree !
It flung and it curled its boughs round me,
They curled and they clung, and my limbs and breast
Felt the throbs of their poison like fire,—and blest
 Was my heart for the pain of the Upas-tree !

O the fierce delight of the Upas-tree !
It burned out the heart and soul from me ;
And the wild pain deadened to dull and slow,
But it held me and would not let me go ;—
    Held in the clasp of the Upas-tree !

O the deadly clasp of the Upas-tree !
My soul was gone—and the limbs of me
Grew into one with those twining boughs,
And I loathèd the ghastly prison house :—
    But nought can save from the Upas-tree !

Now am I one with the Upas-tree,
And scatter poison o'er hill and lea !—
Heart, soul, nor brain is left to me—
Nothing of all I used to be—
    And I am only the Upas-tree.

"PRESIDING EXAMINER."

University of London.

GREY eyes that dream 'neath level brows
  Where high Thought broods with folded wings
And sweet, firm lips, whose smile endows
  The dreariest day with sunlight's springs.
A wreathèd knot of tresses—gold
  In sunlight—in the shadow, brown ;
And, sweeping down in shapely fold,
  The silken rustle of her gown.

Within the quiet, domèd hall,
  Where London fog makes thick the gloom,
And anxious hearts feel very small—
  —We call 't " Examination-room : "—
While quill pens fly across the page,
  And maids of high and low degree
In that first conflict sharp engage—
  Sits silent, sweet and stately, she.

The hood across her shoulders thrown
  Bars with deep gold the murky shade :
The shapely fingers rest upon
  The open book before her laid ;
Grave is her face, and yet, erewhile,
  What time I watched her, there would slip
The ripple of a thoughtful smile
  In glory over cheek and lip.

The swing doors part with motion slow,
 And muffled steps are on the stairs :
And, softly gliding, come and go
 The grey-headed Examiners,
To ask her questions one or two :—
 I think those agèd men were fain—
If so be *she* were there—to do
 Matriculations once again.

And I—whose thoughts are very far
 From travelling Euclid's thorny road—
Am dreaming of the Evening Star,
 And old King Atlas' weary load,
And girls that heard Pythagoras talk,
 And many things ;—as slowly she
Takes up and down her stately walk,—
 The sweetest London B. Sc.

THE SONG OF A SINGER.

"WHENCE comest thou to the Heaven-gate?"
      "Weary and late, weary and late,
I come from wandering up and down,
All unworthy to take the crown."

"Who art thou, so deathly of hue?"
"One who was bidden dare and do—
Who was sent forth as a singer of might
To speak to the earth of love and light."

"Whence are thy raiment and feet so torn?"
"From paths set thick with briar and thorn:
The ways of the world are smooth and fair—
But Christ's own singers may not walk there."

"Singer—how has thy work been done?"
"Ah me! ah me! for the setting sun,
And the truth and beauty that were to be,
And the Face that shall now look sad on me!

"I was still, when He bade me cry aloud,—
My coward head with the throng I bowed,—
Or in wrath and scorn I spake, heart-sore—
And the night is here—no strength for more!"

"O thou singer, enter thou in!
Faithful, thou art of those who win—
Not in vain was the heart's blood poured—
Enter thou into joy of thy Lord!"—

HAUNTING MUSIC.

IT was on a Saturday evening,—
   I walked through the old High street ;
The May had chilled with the twilight,
   But the air was fresh and sweet.

The folks were out at their shopping,
   And many were thronging the stores ;
And loud were the voices and laughter
   As you passed the public-house doors.

Just near the bridge, on the pavement,
   As my homeward walk began,
There stood two strolling musicians,—
   A boy, and an old, old man.

And that wild, chill May evening,
   With a clear sky and no moon,
They stood and played in the twilight
   A wild and wondrous tune.

The instruments they played on,
   And the tune, I do not know,—
But it haunts me still, like voices
   Out of the Long Ago.

Voices wild and weird,
   Glad with a strange, mad glee,
And sadder than ever was wind of death
   Over a desolate sea.

Half of a stern defiance,
 Half of a crushed-down pain,
As of men that march to battle,
 Knowing they come not again.

And that strange, haunting music,
 Whether of joy or woe,
It keeps on thrilling within me,
 And will not let me go.

For the voice of all the Ages
 Under the sun and moon
Came back to me in the High Street,
 With that weird outlandish tune.

THE BALLAD OF THE SHIP "*ELIZABETH.*"

I.

IT was in the tropic midnight,
  The meeting of Life and Death—
She sailed across the Spanish main,
  The ship *Elizabeth*.

Since she ran out of Trinidad
  The days they were but seven,—
Her crew were three-score mariners,
  Gallant lads of Devon.

The night was still, the moon was high,
  The stars were white and calm,
And the low ripple of the wave
  Was like a chanted psalm.

" Lo ! what is that ? " said the captain,
  " Far out upon the lee—
Shapeless, long, and low, and black
  Like a reef upon the sea ? "

Adrian Ward beside him stood,
  True friend in life and death,—
Adrian Ward was master's mate
  Of the ship *Elizabeth*.

Dark-eyed and gaunt was Adrian Ward,
    And his cheek was scored with pain,—
Men said he had suffered for the faith
    On the rack in Spain.

Out of the darkness loomed the shape—
    The ship, she neared it fast—
'Twas but a tangle of weed, said one,
    And one, a drifting mast.

And then they heard a voice that sang
    Athwart the midnight clear—
Sweet! oh! sweet!—the mariners
    Held their breath to hear.

Said the Captain : " Could I hear that voice
    For each day of the seven,
I'd sail on here for evermore,
    And never home to Devon ! "

Sad of face grew Adrian Ward—
    Stept up and took his hand :—
" Never such was good to hear
    By sea or by land ! "

Laughing then he turned from him
    As if in merry strife :—
" Adrian, lad, thou knowest not
    The good there is in life ! "

And lo ! they saw on the floating wrack
    A maiden wondrous fair,
In a robe as bright as the moonbeams white,
    And like wrought gold was her hair.

Dark, dark were her witching eyes,
  And silver-clear her brow,
And sweet her lips as rosebuds red—
  "Say, what maid art thou?"

"Oh! whence and whither drift you so,
  That are so young and fair?"
And never a word she answered—but
  Shook back her golden hair.

She stood among them on the deck—
  Their hearts within them died—
The fairest thing that ever moved
  On land or ocean tide.

Her eyes were soft—her step was light
  As summer dews that fall :—
"I like it not," said Adrian Ward,—
  "But God be with us all!"—

II.

Many and many an evil day,
  With never a cloud or breeze,
They had drifted wearily
  Through the tropic seas.

The sun was burning up above,
  The water-casks were dry ;
The seamen lay, and cursed their pain,
  And waited but to die.

And some they fought like tigers then
  For the last drops of the wine—
And some were maddened in their thirst,
  And drank the bitter brine.

And she laughed, that spirit-woman fair,
  Whose face was like the sun—
Who had witched the hearts of all on board—
  Of every man but one.

For Adrian Ward, the master's mate,—
  His heart was sad within ;
He looked with weary, hollow eyes
  On all that woe and sin.

And madness fell on Gilbert Hay :
  He never heard their cries—
He cared for nought in earth or heaven
  But to look into her eyes.

They sat together on the deck
  With a sail for awning spread,—
And she sang softly ;   .   .   .   and forward lay
  The dying and the dead.

III.

Now on one burning afternoon
  When yet three more had died—
Then it was Adrian Ward rose up,
  And stood by the captain's side.

"True friend to me wast thou, Gilbert Hay,
  Ever in word and deed,—
And I love thee far too well this day
  To fail thee in thy need.

"For never before didst thou, God wot,
  Stand in such peril sore—
Thou art casting away both life and soul,
  And the lives of many more."

And the captain—when he heard him speak,
  Died in his heart all grace—
He lifted up his strong right hand
  And smote him in the face.

Never word said Adrian Ward—
  Both hands dropped by his side,—
One moment Gilbert looked in his eyes
  And wished that he had died.

And then her arm was round his neck—
  Her lips to his cheek were prest :—
He drew his good sword from his side
  And stabbed him in the breast.

Down on the deck fell Adrian Ward,—
  Stricken to death moaned he,
"O Christ in heaven! have mercy now
  On this ship's company!"—

Low on his knees the captain lay
  Prone in his agony—
"Adrian! Adrian!—Christ! O God,
  Have mercy upon me!"—

And at that bitter cry, a sound
  Of hollow laughter died—
It was as though a beam of light
  Fled over the ship's side.

IV.

"O Adrian! Adrian!" so he moaned—
  The curse snapt in his breast;—
The dead man's face was beautiful,
  As he lay there at rest.

Down to the westward flaming,
  Sank the pitiless day—
He rose and he staggered forward
  Where the dead and the dying lay.

Oh! and one looked up at him
  With haggard eyes and brow—
Robin Heard of Exeter :—
  "Captain! is it thou?"

He bowed his face upon his hands
  With a bitter, bitter cry—
"All these lives upon my head!—
  A sinful man am I!"—

He drew his knife across his wrist—
  He felt the red drops flow :—
"Drink!—there is no other way   .   .
  God help us in our woe!"

And he, scarce knowing what he did,
  With burning lips drank on—
Then looked into the captain's face,
  And knew what he had done.

And he : " I have sinned, God knoweth !—
  No pardon is for me ;—
But it may be my life can buy for these
  Help in their misery ! "—

Beside another dying man
  He knelt upon his knee,—
" 'Tis not enough for all," he said—
  " But some may savèd be ! "

Then lo ! a rushing in the sky—
  A roaring on the main—
A darkness o'er the moon—and swift
  Came down the blessed rain.

And the South-west filled the drooping sails
  And lashed the main to foam,
And swift the ship *Elizabeth*
  Sped on her way for home.

They drank, and felt their life come back,
  And hope for mortal dread—
But Gilbert Hay with folded hands
  Lay still beside the dead.

The flying moon-glints touched his cheek
  And lit his yellow hair,—
The passion and pain had left his face,
  And utter peace was there.

They gathered round him—" He is dead ! "
The muffled whispers fell,—
And some of them said,—" He died for us ! "
And some, " He sleepeth well ! "

And Robin Heard of Exeter,
As he held him on his knee,—
" Captain, oh ! captain ! would to God
That I had died for thee ! "—

EDEN WATER.

IN the level light of the golden gloaming
  Down the sands she came ;
Far, far out were the tide-waves foaming,
  Westward all aflame ;
Where the green river rushes for ever
  Down to the northern sea,
She crossed the shallows of Eden Water ;
  Bonnie Marion Lee !

The tide is out and the river's flowing
  Covers not bare, white feet ;
Oh ! but the winds are soft in their going,
  Sunlight ever is sweet !
Lilting a tune to herself as she stept,
  Merrily aye went she ;
Brown, brown eyes that had never wept :
  Bonnie Marion Lee !

A wild-rose spray, and a handful of gowans,
  And one rose in her hair !
The gate stands open beneath the rowans
  She never entered there !
Who can tell when the wild waves caught her ?
  None to save or see—
The eddies are swift in Eden Water,
  Woe for Marion Lee !

KEEPING TRYST.

THE clouds from the south-west drifting
    Are rushing mountains of snow,—
The moon rides high in the heaven,
    And I know that I must go.

Oh ! where is it you are going ?
    Who calls through the mirk and the mist ?
The winds and the waters are calling,—
    And I may not do as I list !

When the hollow skies are sounding
    With the South-West's rush and roar,—
When the night is a mass of shifting gleams,
    How can I stay from the shore ?

Oh ! stay not to bind the shoe to the foot,
    Stay not to glove the hand !
There's a tryst that must not be missed to-night
    Betwixt the sea and the land.

Bare the head to the airs of heaven,
    And let the locks stream free,
And down, down, through the silent street
    To the Links and the shadowy sea.

Oh ! whither away ?—oh ! whither,
    While the dew lies damp on the sod ?
I'm away to keep my tryst to-night
    With the waves, and the winds of God !

There's a white reef glimmers ghostly
   O'er the ledges black and low,
And the winding pools betwixt them,
   Where the wrack and tangle grow.

Smooth and quiet the water
   Under the cliff-side lies,
With a faint, uncertain glimmer
   Like the gleam in a mermaid's eyes.

Turn away from the lights of the city—
   Look out over the sea!
Look at the driving clouds, as white
   As the robes of the ransomed be.

The south wind scatters and rends them
   Into clefts of deepest blue,
And over the waters in glory
   The white full moon looks through.

Oh! dead men drowned in the waters
   From the ships of long ago—
Oh! wild witch-women whose souls went out
   In the reek and the fiery glow :—

Is it you that are about me
   Whispering to left and right?
Are ye keeping tryst with the wild winds
   Of the Equinox to-night?

K

A MOURNFUL BALLADE OF THE LONDON UNIVERSITY EXAMINATIONS.

Cy est escripte la Complayncte d'ung povre Hère ki fust espluchez & eschoua misérablement ès Examens.

A BLIGHT, a distraction, and terror
  Came over my life long ago :—
And the cause of my failure and error
  I'll tell you as far as I know.
Alack ! for I am but a stunned one—
  No hope for the great B.Sc.
And O, and alas ! but the London
  Matric. was the ruin of me !

I racked my poor brain with Mechanics,
  And daily at Euclid did grind ;—
I was constantly subject to panics
  When Algebra came to my mind,
But, shocking to say, I got none done ;—
  The Metamorphoses you see,
Got muddled with surds,—and the London
  Matric. was the ruin of me !

With grammar my brain was quite dizzy—
  I dreamed of equations all night,—
For visitors I was too busy
  (And also too much of a sight) ;
Ah ! never has Carmelite nun done
  A penance more cruel to dree !
Yet, after those six months, the London
  Matric. was the ruin of me !—

L'Envoi.

Friends, Algebra leave it not undone—
  Nor careless of Chemistry be !
Scorn none of your subjects : the London
  Matric. was the ruin of me !

"ICH ABER . . . ."

A WHILE my heart has been anchored,
But she tugs at her anchor-chains,
She is weary of the harbour
With its quiet pleasures and pains.

Sweet, sweet is the quiet life
And the shelter of the home—
But O! for the dashing billows
And the flying sheets of foam.

Out of the East the horsemen
Came with the lance and bow,
Out of the sandy deserts,
Out of the steppes of snow.

Out of the East my fathers
Came in the days of old—
Out of the sandy deserts,
Spearmen and archers bold.

And their spirit is within me,
I feel when the winds are high—
And O! for a steed in the desert!
For I must wander, or die.

And O! for the ship of the Norsemen,
And the blinding, drifting foam—
For the sons of men are my brothers,
And the wide world is my home!

And O ! for the crashing cannon,
    And the clash of swords at strife,
And the loyal love of comrades,
    And the fierce red wine of life !

For the North wind and the South wind—
    The iceberg and the floe,
And the grim and lonely waters!
    Where the great whales come and go !

For the East wind and the West wind,
    And the mountain-peaks of snow,—
The palms, and the starry passion-blooms
    In the land of Mexico !—

Oh ! why did the blood within me
    Throb strong from a wandering race,
If I must grow forever
    In one still dwelling-place ?

Oh ! why did God send me wandering,
    While my childish eyes were dim,
O'er the wide waste Southern waters
    Where man is alone with Him ?

And these broken visions, these echoes
    That linger in soul and brain   .   .
Can you wonder I am restless
    And long to go forth again ?

IN THE SACK OF ATHENS B.C. 86.

SO long ago !—O golden head !
    O level brows whereon the dread
Of coming years was shadowed !
When with white robes and sandalled feet
The maiden train passed down the street,
She walked among them, fair and sweet,
          My sister Leocorion.

All worthy of thy fairest name
O Athens, fallen from ancient fame,
Were those clear eyes untouched of blame !
Why, when thy doom came down on thee,
The whitest soul of all, did *she*
Drink deepest of thy misery,
          My sister Leocorion ?

So long ago ! yet still I hear
That one sharp scream of mortal fear
Above the brazen din ring clear—
When I, down-beaten to my knee
Struck wildly, blindly, helplessly,
What time the spoilers rushed on thee,
          My sister Leocorion !

One swift flash, just as I went down
Of struggling wrists, and torn white gown,
And grey eyes agonised to stone—
Then all was night . . . the triremes bore
The captives from the Attic shore,
And I have never seen thee more,
　　　　My sister Leocorion.

And now, a rhetor bent and old
A Roman bondslave bought and sold.
I sell philosophy for gold :
But where art thou ?—I dare not say—
I can but hope thy sweet eyes may
Be dark unto the light of day,—
　　　　My sister Leocorion !

SCOONIE HILL, ST. ANDREWS.

May 27th, 1885.

G REEN the hillside—the grass is long,
And the wings of the rushing wind are strong,
And the lark flings down the rain of his song.

Nothing I see, as here I lie,
Save green grass-blades, and the depth of sky,
Where the clouds go drifting, hurrying by.

Glimpses of blue,—and streaming light,
Seaward into the northern night,
Drift-veils of grey and pearly white.

The sea and the city they lie below,—
And the brown-sailed boats that come and go,—
And the great plough-horses toiling slow. . .

. But never a thing I saw or heard,
But the soughing winds, and the sky, and the bird,—
And the grasses about my head that stirred.

IN THE GRAVEYARD.

κἅν ἀπίῃς, τοὖε μοὶ τρὶς ἐπαιάσον ὧ φίλε κείσαι.

THEOCRITUS.

SPEAK to me ! think you I'd be afraid
   If I saw your face before my face now,
With an added depth in the dark eye's shade,
   And a colder whiteness on cheek and brow ?
O my love ! my love that I cherished
   When skies were bright, and when earth was new,—
My love that I love now the light has perished,
   Have I so changed that I could fear *you ?*

Fear you, beloved ? Why should I fear !—
   Though the night be dark, and the wind be shrill,—
And the grey clouds drift, and the sea moans near,
   And the minster towers loom dim and chill ?
What should I fear, in the whole wide world,
   When nothing can 'scape the eye of God—
When the wings of the Eternal Presence are furled
   Over me here, and you under the sod.

Fear—and why ?—This world, it is His,
   And that other strange world that now holds you ;—
Shall we doubt, since each of us loves and is,
   That any marvel of His is true ?
Maybe I'd think there was no God at all,
   Could I once feel sure you had ceased to be :
But I know that you are beyond the wall,
   Though it keep your eyes and hands from me.

I know—I know—but, speak to me, love!
  Will you not come?   I am not afraid ?
What can harm me, or what should move,
  In a world that the holy God hath made !
Matter and spirit—spirit and flesh —
  Who can explain it ? or what do we know ?—
See—the dawn lightens, the dews are fresh !—
  Speak to me once before I go !

———————

A WOMAN'S FAITH.

PASSIONATE—faulty—weak— you say : I grant
it is true.
I am deceived ? nay, verily, I know him better than
you !

You see the man as he is ?   Maybe—and what do I see ?
I see the strength and the glory—the man that *should*
be, and *shall* be.

A man at death-grips with the devil—a man God made
for His own :
And, though I should walk the flames barefoot, that
man shall stand by the Throne.

Blackened, and bruised, and bleeding,—and his strength
is failing fast . . . .
But, O my Love, my Love, thou shalt overcome at last.

On the slippery brink thou art standing ; my arm is
about thee laid—
I have given my soul to God's keeping,—and why
should I be afraid ?

Is thy spirit fainting within thee ? Is thy heart with
the struggle sore ?
I say that he shall not have thee, though he strive for
ever more.

I take in mine arms—I claim thee—thus, now, by this
hand and sign,
The fiend has no power upon thee—henceforth, thou
art God's, and mine.

WENDELGARD.

(*Lake of Constance*—A.D. 920.)

IN her cell the Anchoress
  Night and morning prayed,
On the lonely mountain side,
  Where the wild deer strayed.

No man ever saw her face—
  In the midnight lone,
Hunters, when the moon was white
  Heard her make her moan.

When the mists were on the lake
  In the sunrise calm,
Maidens hearkened, passing by
  To the chanted psalm.

It was a pilgrim from the South,
  Grey and bent and worn,—
He landed at the harbour-mouth,
  And rested 'neath a thorn.

Up and down, by land and lake
  To Buchhorn church they came
The pilgrims and the beggar folk,
  Blind, and halt, and lame.

" Why wait ye thus at the Minster door ? "
  They heard the pilgrim say.
" It is the Lady Wendelgard
  Comes down to church this day."

" Long ago, in foreign lands
  Her lord was slain in fight,—
In the mountains for his soul
  She prayeth day and night."

" There's her boat ! "—-He heard the keel
  Grate upon the sand,
Saw a stately woman step
  Slowly to the land.

Wearily she swept back her veil,
  Her face was wild and worn—
And trembling rose the pilgrim up
  That sat beneath the thorn.

She gave to one, she gave to each,
  With gentle words and wise,—
And each one felt a hallowing
  From the calm of her sad eyes.

And he has thrust his way to her,
  That pilgrim from the South,
And he has clasped her round the neck,
  And kissed her on the mouth.

The burning flush was on her cheek—
  On her lips the cry :—
" Look mine own,—look up, and see
  If it be not I ! "—

Her head is lying on his breast,
  His arms about her twine—
" What ? hadst forgotten me,
  True wife of mine ? '—

THE UNKNOWN SEA.

Θάλασσα ἀθέσφατος.—HOMER.

T HE mist came down with chilling breath—
She sailed the sea that severeth
Betwixt the shores of Life and Death.

Above her head a white bird flew—
The mist was riven—purple-blue
And·deep the sky ;—one star looked through.

She heard thin voices whisper round,
'Mid the grey water's sobbing sound ;
And faces pale of men long drowned

Loomed up on her.   "Go back, while yet
The way is open, ere we let   .   .   .
The dead lie still : the dead forget."

Her steadfast eyes drooped not for dread,
"*And though the dead forget*," she said,
" *Shall I forget, who am not dead?*".

Then bitter laughters hard and low
Rang round her, but she said—"*I know
My Love hath called me, and I go.*"

" Turn back—no help in love or faith :
There shall no soul of living breath
Enter into the land of Death.

" And deemest thou that he shall spare
Thy blue eyes and thy yellow hair—
The red blood in thy cheeks so fair ? "

Her boat rowed on into the night,—
Her golden hair grew thin and white,—
Her clear eyes lost their living light.

The wide grey waters heave and roll
In weary surges round the Pole,—
The bitter chill strikes to the soul.

Her numb hands loose the weary oar—
The star shines overhead no more—
No sound, no light, no hope of shore.

With eyes that all unseeing were
She lay :—the Bird stooped from the air,
And nestled on her bosom there.

The white, white Bird whose breast of hue
Is crimson, deep as blood stains new—
" O Love ! O Love ! but I was true ! "—

BANNERMAN OF THE DANDENONG.

I RODE through the Bush in the burning noon,
   Over the hills to my bride,—
The track was rough and the way was long,
And Bannerman of the Dandenong,
   He rode along by my side.

A day's march off my Beautiful dwelt,
   By the Murray streams in the west ;—
Lightly lilting a gay love-song
Rode Bannerman of the Dandenong,
   With a blood-red rose on his breast.

" Red, red rose of the Western streams "
   Was the song he sang that day—
Truest comrade in hour of need,—
Bay Mathinna his peerless steed—
   I had my own good grey.

There fell a spark on the upland grass—
   The dry Bush leapt into flame ;—
And I felt my heart go cold as death,
And Bannerman smiled and caught his breath,—
   But I heard him name Her name.

Down the hill-side the fire-floods rushed,
  On the roaring eastern wind ;—
Neck and neck was the reckless race,—
Ever the bay mare kept her pace,
  But the grey horse dropped behind.

He turned in the saddle—" Let's change, I say ! "
  And his bridle rein he drew.
He sprang to the ground,—" Look sharp ! " he said
.With a backward toss of his curly head—
  " I ride lighter than you ! "

Down and up—it was quickly done—
  No words to waste that day !—
Swift as a swallow she sped along,
The good bay mare from the Dandenong,—
  And Bannerman rode the grey.

The hot air scorched like a furnace blast
  From the very mouth of hell :—
The blue-gums caught and blazed on high
Like flaming pillars into the sky ;— .   .
  The grey horse staggered and fell.

" Ride, ride, lad,—ride for her sake ! "—he cried ;—
  Into the gulf of flame
Were swept, in less than a breathing space,
The laughing eyes, and the comely face,
  And the lips that named Her name.

L

She bore me bravely, the good bay mare;—
  Stunned, and dizzy, and blind,
I heard the sound of a mingling roar,—
'Twas the Lachlan River that rushed before,
  And the flames that rolled behind.

Safe—safe, at Nammoora gate,
  I fell, and lay like a stone.
O love! thine arms were about me then—
Thy warm tears called me to life again,—
  But—O God! that I came alone!—

We dwell in peace, my beautiful one
  And I, by the streams in the West ;—
But oft through the mist of my dreams along
Rides Bannerman of the Dandenong,
  With the blood-red rose on his breast.—

AFTER THE BATTLE.

PISTORIA, B.C. 62.

CATILINE ! Catiline !—and he is dead !
Look—the good sword is shivered in his grasp.
And the helm cloven through—and here a thrust
Right through the corslet. . . No !—no heart-beat
  there !
No more, no more . . . And I, the last, have left
Just life enough to drag myself beside,
And lay the dear head on my knee, and look
By this faint moonlight once more in his face
Before I die. I call—he cannot hear—
Not tho' one called him with hot, passionate tears,
And fondest words of love—he hearkens not
To any man's or woman's voice. . . How still
His face is—and the scornful curve is gone
From off his lips—the sword-blades have not gashed
That comely face,—undaunted to the last . . .
Rest—rest—shall sleep not come to those poor eyes
That watched so long and wearily of late ?
See—I have closed them, kissed the cold lips down—
I, who alone am left—since he has none,
Sister, or wife, or love, or friend, but me,
The alien slave, who could not even die
To save him. . . . Ah !—he looks again, as I
Remember him that night, when—O my heart !—
I fled from Rufus, and, with dizzy brain,
  Hastening, and failing breath, and staggering feet,

Through the Suburra,—heard the voices come
Nearer, behind,—and round the corner swept
The merry train of revellers, torch in hand,
And Coan-vested singing-girls, their locks
Wreathed with red roses . .   and the loudest rang
His voice in laugh and song. . . . And I was lost
And hunted, desperate, helpless, fell before
His feet, and thought . . . when—O the look his
  eyes
Flashed into mine ! . . . and then he flung his gown
Over my shoulder, and his sword leapt out
As the pursuers panted up the street . . .
Yes !—that was he—he that is lying there,
With dust and blood of battle on the curls
That once were shining soft with eastern nard,
When Myrtalis' white fingers used to twine
Amid their blackness. . . . 'Twas these eyes flamed
  out
Upon the bloodhounds . . . now they are not
  fierce,—
And these still lips,—'twas they that laughing said—
" So long as I am safe—why so art thou ! "
And slipt his arm through mine. . .   Where art
  thou now ?
I have not left thee. . . . I will come to thee !
Thou canst not hear me speak—thou dost not feel
Mine arms about thee—never, never more
Will hunger hurt thee, thirst, or cold, or pain,
Or cruel words of men. . . .
                        See—all around—

These loved him well enough to die for him !
They might have lived—the Senate gave the choice.
But no—they would not leave him ! . . .
                    Is it still here ?
Yes—here—the left arm, just above the wrist—
That was a dagger-thrust he got, that night,
Fighting for me. . . . And, but two nights ago,
I kissed it—and he laughed his laugh of old,
We had not heard for many months—" Why now—
Hast not forgotten that ? " *Could* I forget ?
O heart—O hand that saved me !—Never one,
Not Manlius, nor Lentulus, that died
At Rome, they say—though Roman-born, and free
Has loved thee more than I ! . . .
                    O Catiline !
I have no god to call upon, but thee—
And thou art gone ! . . . The stars reel in the sky—
There is a rushing in mine ears—I think
The end is come. . . . I am coming—Catiline !

BALLADE OF A GARDEN.

MEXICO, 1865.

W HITE calla-lilies stood up in the sun,
 And great white roses in many a spray
Over and over the bower did run—
 Was it December or was it May?
 All seemed the same in that garden gay,
In Tacubaya long ago.
 " *Where's Tacubaya?*" do you say?
It is a village in Mexico.

I do not know the name of the tree
 Whose striped bell-blossoms would swing and sway,
Crimson and yellow,—the honey bee
 Hung in their sweet depths all the day.
 The humming-birds' 'twixt those blooms would play
Like emerald fire-sparks to and fro—
 " *Where's Tacubaya?*"—do you say?
It is a village in Mexico.

Oh ! the sunny porch, with its screen of rare
    Blossoms blue as the tropic day,—
And the well where the tortoise lived, and where
    Black-eyed Antonia filled the clay
    Pitchers :—and Madre Juana grey,
Crooning over the embers low ;—
    " *Where's Tacubaya?*" do you say ?
It is a village in Mexico.

Envoi.

Friend, who have listened to me, I pray,
    If ever any should want to know
Where Tacubaya is, you'll say—
    " *It is a village in Mexico.*"

THE ADVENTURE

OF *ADHERBAL* THE CARTHAGINIAN

When he sailed in the ship TANITH *through the* PILLARS OF HERCULES *and into the unknown regions about the coast of* LIBYA.

ADHERBAL, Master-Mariner,
  At Carthage on the quay,
Sat and watched the quinqueremes
  Standing out to sea.

His beard was long and white,
  And his hawk-eyes black and keen—
"Now tell us, Master-Mariner,
  Of the wonders thou hast seen!"

"We sailed from Carthage out and out
  Before the eastern breeze,
Past Calpe and past Abyla
  Into the unknown seas.

Lads of Zidon and Arvad,
  A brave ship's company :—
First away to the westward,
  Then ever south ran we.

Of the barren lands to the south,
  Where the fire-fountains swell,—
Of the incense-woods, and the burning drouth,
  It were long to tell.

But we came into an island
  Where a great fire flamed on high,
Far-shining for a terror
  Into the midnight sky.

And we heard athwart the forest
  The voice of crying long drawn,
And the noise of flutes and cymbals,
  And in fear we waited the dawn.

At dawn we saw a mountain-peak
  Rise white, and calm, and grand,—
No voice of man or beast was heard
  In all that lonely land.

Bostar and Bomilcar,
  Mago, Maharbal and I,
We went ashore in the shallop—
  Now, ye may say I lie, —

But the woods were all of spice-trees
  And the rocks of crystal fair,
And the bright brooks flowed o'er pebble-stones
  That sparkling jewels were.

The deer came down upon the strand,
  With quiet, wondering eye,—
The wild doves brooded on their nests
  And never sought to fly.

And where the slanting sunlight fell
  Across a level lawn,
'Mid the white lilies breast-high grown,
  There stood a snow-white fawn.

The creature stood and looked at us,
  And nought of ill might know ;
But, ere I saw it, Mago sent
  An arrow from his bow.

The white fawn cried, and turned and fled
  With the arrow in her breast—
I followed after through the wood
  With Mago and the rest.

Through many a tangled woodland way,
  Over brook and stone,
We came to where a woman sat
  On a rock alone.

White the robe that rippling flowed
  To her golden sandals down,—
White her arms and bosom were,
  As the snow on Lebanon.

And night-black were the drifted locks
  That fell about her knees,—
Clear and dark her eyes, as night
  Over summer seas.

Never maid so clear a brow,
  No shadow could eclipse ;—
Never mother had such eyes
  Or such loving lips.

And at her feet a lion couched,
  And on her shoulder bare,
Sat a young eagle in his might,
  And nestled in her hair.

Out flashed her eyes on us
  With a wrath divine :
" Ye bear rule in your own lands—
  Touch not this of mine !

" There are groans and wailing and sorrow,
  In the lands where men are known :—
O ye sons of madness and folly,
  Leave me this isle of mine own ! "—

We stood together, stricken men—
  Our hearts might hardly beat ;—
But young Maharbal broke from us,
  And flung him at her feet.

He could not speak, his tears ran down :—
  She smiled with tender grace—
She took his head between her hands
  And kissed him on the face.

We left the isle and northward sailed,
    And saw the pillars gleam ;—
But young Maharbal evermore
    Walked as in a dream.

He smiled to himself, and spake strange words—
    But at last he had his desire:
They found him dead before the shrine
    Of Melkarth's temple in Tyre.

EPILOGUE.

HELD by the arm of God I leant
    Over the fathomless, great abyss,—
The lights and the cloud-wracks whirled and blent—
    The voice of the waves that moan and hiss ;
The long blue lightnings like serpents curled,
    The thunders sobbed out along the air—
And I looked, and I watched them, world on world
    Passing, each in his order there.

Dark and dizzy the great gulf lay,
    Black as the depth of a midnight sky,
And the atom-shoals drifted by on their way,—
    And there,—a speck in the void, hung I !—
O fathomless depth ! O great gulf blind !
    How can man born of woman bear
To feel thy vastness rush on his mind,
    And not be crushed into nothing there ?

There, in face of the awful Deep.—
    "What am I—I should dare to be ?"
And it drove me, into the gulf to leap—
    Then I turned my face, O my God, to Thee !—
Was it more than a man should dare ?   Ah me !
    If to make us Thou didst not scorn,
Why were it so unworthy Thee
    To guide each soul of us, morn by morn ?

EPILOGUE.

Maybe the world had been no worse
Had I leapt and sunk in the great gulf wide :—
Some say 'tis the self-conceit that's our curse
Makes us think that others care we have died.
But O—from our Mentors we turn the head—
Helpless and broken, we cry to Thee!
Thou, who didst call us out of the dead
Void, wouldst care if we ceased to be !

This I know, that in fearless vision
I clasped Thy knees, as a mortal may,—
And the swing and sway of my thoughts' collision
In peace the utterest passed away.
Hearing of lies, to the Truth I turned—
Blinded with darkness, I looked to the sky,—
And knew of the rapture undiscerned.   .   .   .   .
Alone together—my God and I !—

Women's Printing Society, Limited, 21 B, Great College Street, Westminster, S.W.